1866 - 1991

125th

ANNIVERSARY

Anne Leo Ellis

The
Dragon
of
Middlethorpe

HENRY HOLT AND COMPANY • NEW YORK

First edition
Published by Henry Holt and Company, Inc.,
115 West 18th Street, New York, New York 10011.
Published simultaneously in Canada by Fitzhenry & Whiteside Ltd.,
195 Allstate Parkway, Markham, Ontario L3R 4T8.

Library of Congress Cataloging-in-Publication Data
Ellis, Anne Leo.
The dragon of Middlethorpe / Anne Leo Ellis.
Summary: When rumors of a dragon and its treasure stir up greed
and fear in the medieval village of Middlethorpe, thirteen-year-old
Kate is forbidden to join the dragon hunt because she is a maid, so
she takes matters into her own hands.
ISBN 0-8050-1713-5
[1. Dragons—Fiction.   2. Middle Ages—Fiction.   3. Sex role—
Fiction.]   I. Title.
PZ7.E467Dr   1991
[Fic]—dc20   91-14670

Henry Holt books are available at special discounts
for bulk purchases for sales promotions, premiums,
fund-raising, or educational use. Special editions
or book excerpts can also be created to specification.

Printed in the United States of America
on acid-free paper. ∞

1 2 3 4 5 6 7 8 9 10

Acknowledgments

My profound gratitude to Brenda Bowen for her assessment of the original manuscript; to Simone Kaplan for her uncompromising and imaginative editing; to Michael Martine for his inspired suggestions; to Monica Leo and William Ellis for their unfailing support.

For William

Contents

The Dragon
of Middlethorpe

1

The Apothecary Shop

It was St. Margaret's Day. Kate looked around the empty market square, clutched her long skirts, and ran across the cobbles. Her mother would be horrified at such unseemly behavior in a maid of thirteen, but Kate didn't care. It was such a glorious morning! As she turned into Spice Alley, she looked up at the tall narrow houses with their pointed roofs. It seemed to her the whole of Middlethorpe looked scrubbed and sparkling for Daisy's name day. Windows glittered in the sun. Shafts of light between the buildings illuminated the winding street and the wares of its shopkeepers, displayed on countertops in the open air. Kate darted back and forth among clumps of housewives and tradesmen, stopping only to play with some mangy dogs, old friends, who yelped joyfully when they caught sight of her.

But there was no time for play, Kate reminded herself sternly, pushing away assorted dusty paws and wet noses, steeling herself against several pairs of reproachful eyes. She dare not stop longer! Besides, though the errand at Master Clement's was for her mother, Kate had important business of her own. But each time before, when she had tried to speak, her throat contracted and her tongue turned into a huge lump. Perhaps today she would be brave enough to say something. She ran quick fingers through her always-tangled curls and smoothed her skirts, disordered from tussling with the dogs. Kate's heart pounded. If only her nerve would not fail this time!

She stopped for a moment to calm herself, admiring Master Clement's beautiful sign which swung gently in the breeze. It was the painting of a large mortar and pestle on a green background. Master Clement had explained to her that the green stood for the herbs and grasses he pounded in his mortar to make his medicines. Master Clement was the only apothecary for miles around, and everyone said he had more knowledge than the most learned doctor in London or Paris.

As she stepped into the cool, dim shop, Kate was engulfed by the pungent aroma of a hundred medicinal plants and herbs. A large stone mortar, model for the sign outside, stood on one side of a high oaken counter. On the other side rested a set of delicate brass scales. The walls were lined with a bewildering array of jars, bottles, and boxes filled, Kate knew, with countless varieties of oils and ointments.

Master Clement spent many days in the woods

and fields around Middlethorpe gathering the roots and berries and barks, the leaves and grasses and fungi from which his medicines were derived. Kate loved to watch him at his work. Best of all were the times when he allowed her to help, weighing out powders and potions on the scales, or pounding berries and roots in the large stone mortar. Then he would tell stories of the herbs he had gathered, and of the strange lands where his spices grew. Kate thought that Master Clement's shop was the most wonderful place in the world. But at the moment it was silent and seemed empty.

"Master, are you there?"

"One moment, one moment." A head appeared over the high counter, followed by narrow shoulders covered with a dusty, herb-stained robe. The hair was gray and hung in wispy strands. The face was pale and delicate, with a network of fine wrinkles. "My daughter, what a pleasant surprise! How can I serve you?" Kate smiled up at him, startled as always by his height.

"Mother wants ginger and black pepper," she said, holding out a small fabric pouch. "She thinks Father may be home today from Flanders. She's preparing a feast for him."

"That is indeed good news," said the master, taking a jar from a nearby shelf. "And I shall be glad to get my spices." He poured precious black peppercorns into the pouch and added several dried roots of ginger. "Here you are, my daughter."

"Master, I came for another reason." Now! she thought to herself. Ask him!

"What is it? What do you wish to know?" Master Clement looked at her with kind, questioning eyes.

"Master, do you know Tim? The glassblower's apprentice?"

"Indeed I do! One of the finest young craftsmen in the district."

Kate relaxed. It was a good beginning. "Master, Tim loves glass, and is happiest when he is working with it. He told me being an apprentice is the greatest joy he could ever have dreamed of."

"That does not surprise me," replied the apothecary. "If one truly loves one's craft, nothing is more satisfying than the plying of it. I remember my days of apprenticeship with equal pleasure."

Now was the moment! Kate took a deep breath. "Master, I love herbs and healing as Tim loves his glass. I want to learn about them."

"That, too, does not surprise me," replied the apothecary. "It is a love you inherit from your Grandmother Kate. None other in these parts was as well-versed as she. But you already know a good deal, my child."

"Only what I have learned from watching you. Mother has an herb garden, but cares for naught save her kitchen plants. Master, I want to learn. Really learn. Not bits of this and that, as one does without thought. I want to become your apprentice." Kate stopped for breath. She had done it!

Master Clement stared. "My apprentice!"

"Why not? If Tim can be an apprentice, why can't I?" She looked at him anxiously, overwhelmed by a terrible thought. "Do you think I'm not clever enough?"

"Clever enough? I cannot think of another maid as clever."

"Well, then?" Kate clenched her hands and felt her face grow hot. "Is it perhaps because I am a maid?"

"Be calm, my child," said the apothecary. "Your grandmother was one of the most accomplished herbalists in the district, though she never had a day of formal training. But it is true that I have not known a maid to serve an apprenticeship." He stroked his chin reflectively. "And yet, why not? We live in new and different times." He lapsed into thought. Kate looked at him and held her breath. At last he spoke. "Why not, indeed? If noblewomen in Paris can learn to read, why should I not have a maid as my apprentice?" He chuckled. "Let me think on it, my daughter. It is a strange notion." He smiled and added, "But one I do not find distasteful."

"Oh, Master!" Kate was dizzy with joy. With relief. "Oh, I'll work hard and learn all you teach me!" She remembered the heavy volumes of herbal lore stored in his private living quarters. "Could I learn a little about reading, as well?"

"Perhaps, my child," said the master, still smiling. "Perhaps."

Kate was triumphant. Finally she had asked, and

the master had not said no! Suddenly, with horror, she remembered the time. "I must go. It will soon be time for Daisy's feast. Will you be there as well?"

"Alas, no," replied the apothecary. "Two of the baker's little ones are ill and require a potion." He rummaged beneath the counter. "Later I shall send Daisy a sugar cone, but it must wait until your father arrives with my new supply. As for the other matter we discussed," he added with a reassuring nod, "we shall speak of it again."

As she made her way down Spice Alley, Kate felt she was floating. She knew that she would still need to persuade her father and mother of the plan. And it would not be easy, for Kate knew her father had no taste for his daughter's adventurous ideas. And her mother, absorbed with house and garden, could not fathom that a maid might yearn for something else. Fortunately, reflected Kate, they both thought more highly of Master Clement than of anyone she knew.

In a moment she was back in the great market square, surrounded by the grandest buildings in Middlethorpe. Kate loved the square, its large and splendid Guildhall, and the even more magnificent Cathedral. She paused for a moment to watch the stonecarvers at work on the figures of saints near the great doorway, and to marvel at the huge round opening that someday would hold Tim's rose window. With a slight shudder she passed the stocks, today fortunately without an occupant. Kate hated it when some poor wretch was forced to sit for hours with arms and legs clamped into that dreadful contraption.

Over her shoulder she caught a glimpse of Simkin and his dancing bear in the shadow of the Guildhall. She waved, but they did not see her, and reluctantly she continued on her way. Why were they here so soon? Kate wondered. Simkin came each year without fail for the Middlethorpe Fair, but it was still early. Her father was not even back from Flanders. At the thought of Master Simon's return, she started to run. Her mother was at home waiting for the spices, and Kate should have delivered them long before now. Besides, she still needed to gather flowers for Daisy's feast!

2

A Rumor of Dragons

Kate breathed deeply of the fragrant air, heavy with the scent of mint, wild flowers, and fresh summer grass. How beautiful the meadow was! Like the precious tapestry in the Guildhall—rich emerald green scattered with the sharp gold and white of a million daisies and buttercups, framed on the horizon by the dark line of the forest. She looked around. Everything was perfect! The beautiful day, the flower-strewn meadow, the outcome of her long-dreaded talk with Master Clement. With a burst of sheer joy Kate flung out her arms, spun around wildly, and collapsed dizzy and laughing in a tangle of skirts and grasses.

She sat up and looked back at Middlethorpe, spread over a shallow rise, the Cathedral's tower soaring above the massive wall that surrounded the town. Below, where Beechwood Brook ran through the fields, lay Daisy's tiny village. The weathercocks of Middlethorpe glittered in the sun, and the smoke of a hundred chimneys rose lazily into the cloudless sky. Kate could almost smell the simmering dinners, and her stomach growled, reminding her of Daisy's feast and that there would be wonderful things to eat! She sprang to her feet and turned her attention firmly to the daisies.

They grew thick all around her, gold and white, their slender stalks almost hidden in fresh young grass and fragrant mint. Swiftly she gathered an armful. Daisy was a nickname for Margaret, and today was St. Margaret's Day. Daisies for Daisy! Kate's gift would be masses of the flowers that bore her friend's name.

Hurrying through the fields, Kate caught sight of Beechwood Brook as it threaded its way to the village. On its banks the fullers were pounding and scrubbing mounds of woolen cloth, while masses of sheep tumbled over each other in their eagerness to drink. Beyond, almost hidden by a grove of ancient oaks, were the glassblowers. Kate wondered if Tim was there. She loved to watch him wield his blowpipe, shaping bubbles of blue or green, scarlet or purple, or of shining crystal that reflected all the colors of the rainbow. Suddenly she remembered that Tim would be at Daisy's feast to play his flute for the dancing. She could tell him about her talk with Master Clement!

Reaching the village, she hurried past the straw-thatched cottages, most of them empty, their occupants out in the fields or already at the celebration.

"Miss Kate!"

Daisy waved from the little cottage garden. She was small, with trusting blue eyes, and the child beside her looked like a tiny version of his mother. Robin. Though usually dressed in coarse homespun, today Daisy wore a sky blue gown that matched her eyes, every strand of hair hidden by a crisp white kerchief. Once when Kate had objected, Daisy had been shocked. "Miss! I'm wed, and a mother. It's not proper I should leave my hair uncovered for everyone to see! Wait till you're wed," she had added. "Then you'll understand."

Kate knew she'd never understand, but that was for another time. Right now nothing mattered except the festive day.

"For you." Kate gave the flowers to Daisy and bent down to hug Robin.

"Oh, Miss, they're beautiful! And just wait till you see what I have to put 'em in! Go out with the others," she said to Kate, pointing to the back garden, then hurried back into the cottage, little Robin trailing after her.

In the shade of a towering elm stood a table heaped with good things to eat, and leaning against the massive trunk or seated on the grass were the guests. Kate spotted Brother Luke, clad in a robe of coarse brown homespun belted with a heavy rope, his tonsured hair forming a ragged fringe around his shaven head. He was deep in conversation with Tim, who stood rumpling his shock of flaming hair, his gentle face deep in thought. Wat, the blacksmith, was on all fours giving two of his daughters a horse ride. Harry, Middlethorpe's innkeeper, held out his tankard to arthritic old Bet, who poured him a measure from an earthenware pitcher.

Someone grabbed Kate by the shoulder. "Sister! What kept you?"

She looked up into the smiling face of a boy not much older than herself. With close-cropped dark curls and gray eyes so like her own, there was no mistaking the connection.

"Geoffrey! Don't you remember? I went to pick flowers for Daisy."

Suddenly Kate heard the sound of fiddle and flute. "Look, they're starting to dance!" She watched the tall figure of Daisy's husband come through the garden, Robin perched high on his shoulder. He spun the little boy around until he was dizzy and laughing, then set him down under the great tree.

"Miss Kate!" he called. "A dance with old Rob, the gatekeeper!"

Kate jumped to her feet and off they went. She caught a fleeting glimpse of Tim, head bent over his flute, red hair aflame in the sun, and wished she were dancing with him. Soon everyone whirled and stamped in rhythm to the music, even Brother Luke. Finally they formed a large circle around the old elm, moving faster and faster, suddenly letting go hands and dropping, breathless and laughing, to the ground.

"Oh," gasped Jen, the plump and pretty wife of Wat, "I haven't danced like that since round the maypole in Lord Hugo's meadow!"

"It was a jolly dance," said Harry, carefully lowering his bulk to the ground. "You do well on that flute," he called to Tim. "You too, fiddler!"

"Cake! Cake!" Little Robin spied his mother coming from the cottage, bearing a vast pastry covered with apples and nuts.

Then everyone gathered to eat all the good things on the table. There were Daisy's cakes, stewed fruits and nuts, fish salads, egg dishes, and puddings made of curdled milk and spices.

"Tomorrow it's back to oats and cheese," said Wat, his mouth full of honey tart. "But I'll pretend my oatcake is stuffed with apricots and rolled in sweet sugar."

Daisy took some empty platters from the table and replaced them with her birthday surprise: a large jug of glowing purple glass filled to bursting with Kate's daisies. "Isn't it beautiful, Miss?" She looked at Tim. "There was no need," she said with a radiant smile, and hurried back to the cottage for more cakes.

"I'm glad I could make it for her," said Tim to Kate. "We all know Daisy's love of flowers."

Kate ran her finger along the jug's smooth curves, and straightened a flower. "I didn't know you could make such things, Tim," she said admiringly.

"We had pigment left over from a section of the

rose window," he explained. "The master said I might have it." He looked at her shyly. "With those daisies, it looks as if you and I had planned it."

Kate felt her face grow hot; she could tell she was blushing. "I knew nothing," she said, but suddenly the day was even more wonderful. "Tim, this morning I saw Master Clement, and . . . Daisy! What is it?" she exclaimed as Daisy rushed back out of the cottage.

"Oh, Miss! Something terrible! Fife's outside."

And, indeed, just rounding the cottage was the itinerant peddler who traveled the length and breadth of the region with his faithful old mule. Where was Peterkin? Kate wondered, for the peddler and his animal were inseparable. Fife wore his usual ragged surcoat and ancient cap pulled low over unkempt locks. His eyes were wild.

"Fife! Whatever's wrong?"

The peddler's usual whining, petulant manner was gone. His face reflected nothing but terror.

"A dragon, Miss! There's a dragon loose!" Fife looked around. "He could come swoopin' down on us any moment!"

Everyone stared at him, too stunned for speech.

"Don't you understand?" The peddler's voice shook. "The dragon's returned! The dragon of Middlethorpe's come back!"

"You! Peddler!" Rob had hurried over at the sound of the commotion. "What brings you here? This is a feast, an' no one asked for you."

"There's a dragon loose, Gatekeeper! I've come to warn you!" The peddler began to shiver, his eyes darting in all directions. "It was terrible!" Fife pulled a filthy rag from his tunic and wiped his face. "I was comin' from Thornleigh. I'd settled to sleep by the side o' the road. You know, where it runs beside the woods. Suddenly there was smoke an' fire. In great huge spurts—like a dragon breathin'." He looked around at his listeners. "There was a terrible stink in the air." His eyes looked mad, staring. "The devil is after us! That monster's Satan himself!"

"What nonsense you talk!" exclaimed Harry. "It's naught but the ale in that miserable body of yours! I've seen you drunk too often to count!"

"It was the monster!" shrieked the peddler. "I know it was! You should a' been—" He stopped. "The stink! You never smelled such a stink! An' flashes of light dartin' all around." He wiped his sweating face. "You should've been there! It was just like last time!"

"What do you mean, last time?" Kate's stomach began to churn. But she knew what he meant. She had heard the stories all her life.

"There was a whooshin', Miss, a whooshin' an' sweepin' through the air, like the sound an' shadows of huge bats!" Shudders racked Fife's body. "My Peterkin shivered an' screamed with fright." He looked up at a gaunt mule that was making its way along the side of the cottage. "Here, my darlin'. I'm here!"

The mule shambled up the path and nuzzled its owner. "We know what we saw, don't we, my pet?" Fife scratched the mule behind the ears and looked defiantly at the others.

"You were dreamin', Peddler," said Rob, swinging up little Robin, who had come running after his father. "There's been no dragon in these parts for years."

"Why should we believe you?" challenged Wat brusquely. "You're always drunk, and the whole district knows it! The innkeeper's right!"

"For that matter," interrupted Jen, "when have you ever told truth? You with your shoddy wares—" She stood with her arm around the distraught Daisy. "He wants naught but make a scene, and be important."

The peddler looked at Jen with bloodshot eyes. "Call me what you like. I'm tellin' you truth. You'll yet wish you'd heeded my warnin'." He shivered again.

Kate listened with pounding heart. Her throat was tight, and her head whirled with all the old thoughts. Could the peddler be believed? Was it possible that after all these years the dragon of Middlethorpe was back? But no. Be calm, she told herself. For the love of the saints, be calm. Jen and the others are right about Fife. A troublemaker, and a dishonest and drunken one at that! She pulled herself out of her thoughts.

"It's the talk of a fool!" exclaimed Rob.

"That's as may be," said old Bet, "but listen to the peddler."

"There've been strange rumors from time to time," said Wat thoughtfully, looking at Bet. "Who's to say? Maybe the peddler's right. What if that monster's been in those caves on the other side of the forest all this time? Dragons are supposed to live forever."

"Folks said the dragon stole a little girl!" It was one of Wat and Jen's small daughters, and she spoke more in wonder than fear.

"They found her later," said Rob, "drowned in a pond. She'd just wandered off by herself."

"But there've been other tales, for sure," said the innkeeper. "Perhaps I was wrong to scorn your words, Peddler."

Daisy let out a wail. "We'll all be killed in our sleep. Especially here, outside the walls! Where's Robin?" She broke free from Jen and ran for the little boy, clasping him in her arms.

Brother Luke touched Kate on the shoulder. "When does Master Simon return?"

Kate looked at him. "Do you believe Fife speaks truth?"

"It may be naught save the peddler's drunken imaginings," answered the friar, "but once such tales spread, people are hard to control. The burgesses will need to know without delay."

"He should be home any moment," said Kate, suddenly longing for her father's solid good sense. "The

Flanders Fair is over, and he needs to prepare for the one in Middlethorpe."

"You haven't heard, Miss?" interrupted the peddler. Some of his petulance had returned, as had the whine.

"Heard what?"

"In truth, I was surprised to see you. With yer pa just home, an' his goods all blackened with fire an' smoke."

Geoffrey broke in. "You saw our father?"

"No, that's to say, I didn't see your pa, but I ran into someone I know who stayed at the Cock 'n Feather in Benningfield last night. He said there'd been a fire, an' that Master Simon'd been there; that his goods were burned and blackened in the flames. He traveled with your pa to Middlethorpe this mornin' before goin' on to Thornleigh."

"But what about the dragon?" exclaimed Daisy. "You said there was a dragon!"

"There was!" exclaimed the peddler. "Like I said! On the road from Thornleigh, and in Benningfield as well. But you'd best go see for yourselves," he added resentfully, looking at Kate. "You'll not believe old Fife." He turned to Bet, who was listening, ale jug in hand, "Goodwife, my gullet could use a wettin'."

Kate and Geoffrey looked at each other. "Let's go!" They bade quick farewells, and set off through the fields toward Middlethorpe.

"Geoffrey! Do you believe the peddler speaks truth?"

"I'd like to!"

Kate gave him a sharp look. Was it possible the dragon had come back? As long as she could remember, she'd heard tales of the terrible dragon of Middlethorpe! Of the time her Grandfather John had not returned from hunting down the serpent deep in the forest. Nine men had gone. No trace of them was ever found, though the woods had been searched for weeks. Kate remembered herself on her father's lap as the grown-ups sat around the fire on winter nights talking of the dragon, while the wind howled outside, tearing at the doors and windows. It had seemed to little Kate that the wind, like the monster, would break into the warm and cozy kitchen to destroy them all.

And now the dragon was back? All of her life Kate had wanted to see him. All of her life she had hoped secretly that he would return. But now she was frightened. Terrified! Not just of the evil monster, but the forest as well. Even when talking with Master Clement, she had thought about the forest. Would he ask her to gather herbs and berries in that terrible, wild place?

People said the dragon lived in caves deep in that very forest. With its ancient trees, its hollows, bogs, and caves, its evil spirits, vicious wolves, and wild boar that lurked in its depths. The young girls of Middlethorpe had been warned never, ever to venture into the forest alone. And Kate had never wanted to!

"Geoffrey! Let's go faster!"

They broke into a run, and in moments had reached the town gate.

3

Clamor for Action

Once inside the walls of Middlethorpe, they ran until they reached a large half-timbered house—their parents' pride—built after a particularly good year in the wool trade. In front, surrounded by a litter of goods, stood a tall bearded man. They rushed into his outstretched arms.

"Father!" How good it was to see him, thought Kate, as he caught them both in an embrace. "Fife told us he saw you. He said there was a fire!"

"Because of a dragon!" said Geoffrey. "Is it true?"

"A moment," said Master Simon, disentangling himself. "First let me look at you!" He held them off at arm's length, studying each in turn. "You've both grown," he said, smiling with delight. "I can't believe it, Geoffrey. You'll soon be as tall as I!"

"Father!" Kate did not hide her impatience. What did it matter how they looked! "Tell us what happened in Benningfield!" She sniffed. "Something smells burned. Are the goods all right?"

"There was a small fire in the stable," answered Master Simon, "but naught to worry about. And most of the goods are fine. But come," he said, opening the door, "let's go inside and see if your mother's ready. Any moment now I'll wake, and find those smells from the kitchen are naught but a dream, and that I'm somewhere on the road in a bug-infested hostelry. Wife!" he called out. "When do we eat?"

A handsome, fresh-faced woman entered the hall, the bunch of household keys at her waist clinking faintly as she moved. "Not long now." She placed a large dish of stewed fruits on the table and tucked a strand of escaping hair back under the crisp white kerchief that covered her head. "Daughter," she said, turning back to the kitchen, "in a moment I'll need your help."

Kate studied her father carefully. Master Simon's beard was still damp from his end-of-journey bath, but how had he looked several hours earlier? Covered with soot no doubt! And the goods upstairs, the same. If only she could see! But there was just one key—the one Master Simon kept with him day and night. And he permitted no one in the attic. Kate was sure she'd caught a whiff of smoke. There was a great deal Master Simon was not telling them. At the thought, her skin began to prickle.

"Look!" Geoffrey was standing in the doorway. "What's Tim doing here? We just left him at Daisy's." He hurried outside, returning a moment later with the young apprentice. "Father, they're setting stink fires tomorrow to keep the dragon at bay. Tim wants me to help."

"Stay and eat with us," said Kate, passing Tim on her way to the kitchen. "It's Mother's special feast for Father." She glanced toward a lute that hung on the wall. "Later you can play us a melody."

"I'd love to stay," said Tim. "And I'll pay for my meal with a song," he added with a grin.

Together with Janet, the young kitchen maid, Kate brought in the steaming platters. Master Simon waved everyone to the table, seating himself at the head in his own carved chair. "M-m-m-m."

He inhaled the rich aroma from a dish of spiced beef that stood directly before him. "There's nothing like this on the road. You cannot imagine how I long for my first bath and my first real meal after a trip!" He lifted his goblet of wine to Goodwife Barbara, who had just entered the hall bearing a large platter of capons in cream. "I salute you, dear wife!"

Tim sat between Kate and Geoffrey, and the food was handed round the table. Janet brought meat pies and an enormous fish in a fragrant sauce. There were fruits and cakes and a delicate almond custard. Kate burned to talk about the day's events, but her mother's firm rule prevailed: no serious conversation at table. She longed to tell Tim about Master Clement, but dared not because of her parents. Besides, today Master Simon's trip was the topic of the meal. Even Geoffrey, who usually gobbled his food as though he

would not see another morsel, almost forgot to eat
as he listened. It was, after all, his greatest wish to
be a merchant like his father, telling his own tales
of adventure on the road and at the great fairs of
Europe.

"I hear of magnificent cathedrals being built in
Flanders and such places, Master," said Tim during
a lull in the talk. "Have you seen them?"

"The one I think more beautiful than any other,"
replied Master Simon, "is the great church in
Chartres."

"A journeyman stonecutter told me of it," said
Tim. "He said the windows were of glass in the rich-
est colors, and cut in most intricate ways." His face
was thoughtful. "If only our windows turn out half
as well!"

"Your journeyman was right," said Master Simon.
"I am not one who concerns himself with matters
of faith, but they stirred my soul."

"Perhaps one day you will see it yourself," said
Goodwife Barbara, smiling at the young apprentice.

Tim had finished a second piece of honey cake,
and Geoffrey was reaching for the last meat pie when
Master Simon pushed back his chair.

"Come into the garden. The moon is almost full,
and the roses are at their sweetest."

Master Simon and Goodwife Barbara sat down on
a bench still warm from the sun. Tim, on the grass
with Geoffrey and Kate, strummed on the lute. Janet
handed around goblets of spiced wine. Thin clouds

moved across the surface of the moon, placing the little group in shadow or silver light. Kate shattered the dreamy mood.

"Father, now tell us. We've eaten, and it's time. What happened at the Cock and Feather?"

"Kate!" Goodwife Barbara's voice was sharp. "Let your father be. It's his first night at home."

"Mother! There may be a dragon loose! We told you what Fife said. And we know something happened in Benningfield, though Father's managed it so none of us can see the goods. And he won't talk!" Kate could feel her face getting hot with frustration. Why would no one talk?

Master Simon took a deep breath. "All right, then. I suppose I must tell you. Fife told the truth. The goods were scorched and some are severely damaged. There was a fire at the Cock and Feather last night."

"I knew it!" Kate's heart pounded. "Father! Was it the dragon?"

"Who can tell?" Master Simon rubbed his forehead. "People thought so. They panicked. Other things happened. A woman had just died of a stomach ailment."

"That's what Janet said!" burst in Kate. "Father, did people think the dragon had poisoned the water?"

Master Simon nodded. His head was bowed, and he continued to rub his forehead.

"What else, Father?" Kate could sense the excitement in Geoffrey's voice.

"The stableman saw shadows flying overhead,"

said Master Simon heavily. "He claims there were tongues of fire in the sky, and strange sounds."

Tim leaned forward eagerly. "Do you think he speaks the truth, Master?"

"I know not what to believe." Master Simon shook his head with weariness.

"Did you see anything?" asked Kate.

"I saw shadows, of course. But I did not think they were of the dragon."

"People in the village say that stink fires will keep the dragon away," said Tim.

"I think we should have a hunt!" exclaimed Geoffrey. "Father could—"

"That's madness, my son! Your father has just come home from a long journey!" Goodwife Barbara, usually so calm and measured, tugged at her kerchief in visible agitation.

"Please." Master Simon placed a soothing hand on his wife's arm. "It's much too soon to say anything until the burgesses have gathered. As for you, Geoffrey," he continued, "no more talk of a hunt at this time! I order you. We must decide what's to be done, of course. But we must keep our heads. We dare not panic."

"Master." Tim's manner was reluctant. "This evening in the village there was already talk of a hunt. And your name was mentioned as leader."

"Me!" exclaimed Master Simon, staring at Tim. "What nonsense is this? What do I know of dragon hunts?"

"They trust you, Master, and they're frightened."

"Father!" exclaimed Geoffrey. "You'd be perfect!"

"I care not for this nonsense about dragons," said Master Simon. "I fear it is the talk of gullible fools. We should be preparing for the fair, not worrying about dragon hunts."

"Pardon, Husband." Goodwife Barbara, once more composed, spoke firmly. "Dragons have wrought fearful destruction. How can you be unmoved?"

"My dear, it's not that I'm unmoved. I know that we may be faced with grave danger. But rushing off thoughtlessly into the forest would be sheer madness."

Goodwife Barbara was silent. Kate knew she was thinking of the last time and of its horrors. She watched as her mother tugged fiercely at the kerchief, and tucked in the ever-escaping strand of hair. Her mother wanted the dragon dead, but could not bear the thought of another hunt. "We must do something!" she exclaimed. "Before it's too late! Dragons have destroyed countless villages and towns. Middlethorpe must not be one of them!"

"What do you think?" whispered Kate to Tim in the silence that followed her mother's outburst.

"My master heard a strange tale." Tim drew closer, his fiery hair in vivid contrast to Kate's dark curls. "It was told him by a man who had been on a crusade in the East. He said a dragon took possession of a well—I think near Jerusalem."

"Oh, tell me," breathed Kate. "Tell all of us."

"It will distress your mother. But I'll tell you softly, if you wish. The dragon took possession of the town's only well, and would let no one draw near."

"What happened? Did the townspeople kill the monster?"

"They could not. The dragon demanded from them a maid in return for water, and they had been forced to give him every maid in town. Except the daughter of the king. Before the dragon demanded her as well, a strange and wonderful thing happened. A knight appeared, clad in armor of purest gold. He rode up to the dragon on a white horse and pierced him between the eyes with his sword. The dragon died instantly, and the townspeople were able to use their well as before."

"Do you think it true?" asked Kate. "What town would give all its young maids to a dragon?"

"Such things are known to happen."

"What do you whisper over there in the corner?" asked Goodwife Barbara.

"Oh, Mother, Tim told me a wonderful tale of a dragon who ate all the maids in a village—"

"Stop!" exclaimed her mother. "Nothing more of dragons! Forgive me, Tim," she said. "Please, give us a song. But not about dragons, I pray you!"

Tim plucked the strings of the lute. "I'll sing a ballad of unicorns. For as the dragon is a symbol of evil, destruction, and death, so the unicorn represents goodness, courage, beauty, and—most of all— love."

Kate leaned against the sun-warmed garden wall. The fragrance of the roses was overpowering, their heavy blooms washed in the moon's silver. The ripple of the music added to her sense of unreality—a sense of aching sweetness. She looked deep into the brightness of the moon, her thoughts drifting to the unicorn—equally strange and remote. Tim had just begun to sing when she was jarred out of her mood by loud voices and shouting, and by Janet running down the path, eyes wide with excitement.

"Master! Harry, from the Golden Goose, and a lot o' men're here to see you. They're bangin' on the door and callin' for you to come out. Listen, Master, you can hear 'em!"

"It's what I said earlier, Master." Tim interrupted his song, instantly alert. "They've come for your guidance."

Master Simon rose swiftly. "Come, Geoffrey. And you, Tim. We'll unbar the door and see what they want." They hurried up the path, Kate close behind them.

"Daughter, stay with me!"

Kate turned around. "Mother. Please! I want to hear."

Goodwife Barbara frowned with annoyance. "It's not fitting that you . . ." She interrupted herself. "Go, then. But don't be in the way."

Kate ran after the others. In the way! No one ever tried to stop Geoffrey! They hurried through the kitchen and to the front door.

"Master! Open up!"

Together they lifted the heavy oaken bar, and the door swung back on its hinges.

"Good evenin', Master. We must speak with you." Several figures crowded around the door, and Kate could see others in the background, their faces and bodies distorted by the light and shadow of the moon-drenched night.

"Friends, what troubles you? It's late, and you should be home with your wives and little ones."

"Master, we must talk with you at once." The large-bellied figure standing in the shadows was Harry, the innkeeper. "These men were at the Golden Goose drinking their evening ale, and there was naught but talk of the dragon. If the monster's loose, we must do something."

"Yes, that's God's truth!" Kate recognized Wat, the blacksmith. "Fife's tale's got us worried. You've always been our friend, so we came to you."

"Have you heard Fife's news, Master?" asked Harry. "And that a woman died in Benningfield? Poisoned by the water?"

"There's two sheep missin' from the castle flocks." Kate thought it was one of Lord Hugo's herders.

"Men, I've heard the news," said Master Simon. "And tomorrow I'll gather the burgesses. Then we shall decide what's—"

"We need action!" broke in Wat. "Those burgesses take forever."

"It's far too soon, good Wat." Master Simon spoke reasonably. Kate looked at Geoffrey. They knew their father well enough to sense the effort he was making to keep his temper in check. "People die from stomach ailments all the time. These are naught but senseless rumors."

"Are they now, Master?" Harry's voice was mocking. "The peddler tells us you had your own troubles in Benningfield. What of that?"

"My wife's afraid," broke in someone from the back. "Her mum tells of a dragon came to their village once. It spouted fire an' smoke somethin' dreadful—"

"Next thing that monster won't stop with the sheep! He'll steal our babes and little ones!"

"An' the water," broke in the sheepherder. "I heard tell of a dragon that poisoned all the rivers an' lakes."

"Master, please. We come to you for help." It was Wat again.

"Men, it's too soon! These rumors began only today. That business in Benningfield could have been anything at all. We must keep our wits. They're not sharpened by even one measure of evening ale." He looked over the group. "And I doubt you stopped with one."

"Don't put us off with such stuff! Else we might have to show our precious leaders what action is." A large figure had shouldered its way to the front, and Kate recognized the harsh angry voice of Jankin, the cobbler. Though he stood in shadow, her mind's eye supplied the powerful shoulders, the massive head that seemed even larger because of the thick hair and fierce black beard. Kate felt a familiar prickle up her spine. The cobbler frightened her.

"Not only burgesses can make decisions about dragon hunts," continued the aggressive voice.

"Are you threatening me, Cobbler?" Kate knew her father's temper was rising.

"Only to say that while the good burgesses of Middlethorpe sit on their hands, the rest of us'll act like men. We'll go hunt this dragon down and kill 'im." Jankin flung out the challenge, and there were shouts of approval.

"A dragon hunt!"

"—protect our wives an' little ones!"

"We want a hunt!"

"Let's kill the monster!"

"—and be done with it!"

"A hunt!"

Master Simon shook his head. "Men, we have a fair to run."

"What is it ye want, Master?" burst out the fishmonger. "Wait 'til that monster devours us all?"

"What good's the fair if folks're afraid to come? The roads to Middlethorpe ain't safe!"

"I'm goin' on my own," shouted the fishmonger.

"Me too!"

"And I!"

"Men, let me speak!" Master Simon's frustration was apparent, but even now his firm voice commanded respect. "Don't rush headlong into the forest. You know little of the woods, and naught of dragon hunting."

"That's why we want you as our leader!" someone shouted.

"Surely you jest!" exclaimed Master Simon. "What know I of dragons?"

"More than any of 'em," whispered Geoffrey, who was standing with Kate and Tim behind the door.

"Master, you may know little about dragon hunting, but you are wise and keep your head." It was Harry.

"He's right," whispered Kate. "But Mother will be distraught."

"Tomorrow I gather the burgesses," said Master Simon. "Harry, you are one, so you will be there. Until then, I pray, hold your peace and don't take dangerous action that you will regret."

"We don't want to wait!" shouted someone.

"Be quiet!" ordered Harry. "We need to talk." The men gathered in the shadows.

"Your father's right," said Tim. "But people don't like to wait. They want to act first and think later."

"Well, I think the men are right," said Geoffrey heatedly. "The sooner the better. And they're right about Father. He's the best!"

"Just see," whispered Kate, her eyes on the huddle of men. Arms waved, fingers pointed, faces showed anger, frustration, and fear. "Look, they're breaking up."

"The men'll do as you say," said Harry when they had reassembled in front of the door. "At least for now. But they're not happy."

"I thank you for your prudence." Kate felt herself crumbling with the relief she sensed in her father. "And I promise we'll speak tomorrow after I've seen the burgesses. But now, I beg of you, go home. It's late, and I am weary from my journey. Good night to you all."

"Let's go," said Harry, "and do what the master says. Have faith in him, men, for a little while longer."

Still arguing, shaking their heads, still not convinced, the men straggled off into the shadows. All except Jankin. "Do what you think best," said the pugnacious cobbler, thrusting his face into Master Simon's. "But be clear about one thing: Jankin, the cobbler, will make his own decisions." He turned abruptly and, joining the others, disappeared into the night.

Kate watched, then helped bar the door. As always, the cobbler made her flesh creep. "What's Jankin going to do? He frightens me."

"Father," said Geoffrey. "Those men are right. You must lead the hunt!"

Master Simon shook his head impatiently. "I have no time for all this panic and hysteria!" he burst out. "We have a fair to run!" He rubbed his eyes.

Kate looked at him closely, and exchanged glances with Tim and her brother. Master Simon's face was drawn with weariness and strain. "Father," she said, "you need to rest."

"Perhaps you're right," said Master Simon. "It's been a long day, and things may look clearer in the morning. Come," he added briskly, conquering his weariness and leading the way through the house. "Let us join your mother in the garden."

— 4 —

A Casket of Unicorn Horn

Kate had taken a candle to her bedchamber and pulled a scrap of parchment from beneath the mattress. It was a crude ink drawing of a dragon, copied by her brother from an illuminated manuscript in the abbey. Geoffrey's teacher, the abbot, said it was the very dragon that had terrorized Middlethorpe, drawn by a monk long since dead. The dragon was long and scaly, and looked rather like a serpent. It had a spiky back and jointed wings like a bat's. Its mouth spouted billows of flame, and revealed row upon row of pointed teeth. "Could it really be you?" Kate ran her finger over the coils of the tail and could almost feel his slithery scales. Was Fife talking about this very dragon?

Kate slipped the picture back under the mattress and pulled the coverlet up around her shoulders. She squeezed her eyes shut and pretended she was in the forest, dark, deep, evil, menacing. She imagined the dragon—something like Geoffrey's drawing, only a thousand times bigger, with scales of a slimy green. And hundreds of times as big as she, who was cowering, in her mind, behind a hazel thicket. The dragon came closer, teeth viciously pointed, throat aflame, tail lashing. She shivered and trembled. She stretched out flat inside the hazel thicket. She was asleep.

When Kate awoke, the sun was streaming through her little chamber window, and she heard voices from the kitchen below. She dressed, splashed water on her face, and struggled briefly with her curls before hurrying downstairs.

"Miss, guess what?" Janet's eyes were like saucers. "They're goin' to make stink fires tonight to scare off that monster."

"Tim says they'll make those fires with all sorts of filth and waste," said Geoffrey, at that moment entering the room with the young apprentice, who had stayed the night.

"What do you mean, filth?" asked Kate.

"Dung, rotten food, old clothing, all sorts of leavings," said Tim. "Everything that smells evil when it burns."

"Will it work?" Kate had her doubts, but what else was there?

"What we really should do," declared Geoffrey, "is go out and kill the monster!" His eyes glowed, and he pranced about flourishing an imaginary sword.

"St. Geoffrey meets the dragon," taunted Kate in disgust. Sometimes her brother was such a fool! "What if all the hunters get lost like last time?"

"Why should they, if someone clever like Father leads the hunt? Tim, would you go?"

"If my master lets me."

"Why don't you ask me?" demanded Kate. "I'm going if there's a hunt."

"You!" Tim and Geoffrey stared at her. "You can't go!"

"Why not? Why shouldn't I?" She faced them defiantly.

"Miss!"

Kate jumped. What if Janet had heard! She'd forgotten all about her.

"There's a woman in Thornleigh with horrible stomach cramps," said Janet. Thank goodness, thought Kate, letting out her breath in relief, Janet hadn't been listening. "Miss! Did you hear? Just like the one in Benningfield! Folks're sure the dragon's poisoning the water hereabouts."

"Last night Father told Harry that people get stomach cramps all the time," said Kate, feeling a shiver up her spine. "But who's to know . . ."

"It's a strange thing about those monsters," said Tim. "I've heard about them all my life, and my master's full of tales about dragon caves and dragon treasure."

"I've always wanted to see one of the monsters!" exclaimed Kate.

"The master's told me about their wings and claws, their scaly coats of green or red, and their huge size."

"At school the abbot's always talking about their

evil nature and selfish, scheming ways," said Geoffrey. "He says thunder and lightning and rain clouds
are naught but dragon's breath!"

"I believe it," said Tim. "I believe those wicked
beasts lurk somewhere in the land."

"Have you ever seen one?" Kate didn't know anyone who had.

"No, but once the master showed me a huge hole.
He said it had been ripped in the earth by a dragon.
That the monster had burst out of the earth like a
blazing torch." Tim rose. "I must go. The master
will miss me."

"I, too," said Kate reluctantly, for she loved listening to Tim, and hated the prospect of her morning's errand. "Father wants me to fetch his boots."
With a parting grimace, she left to find her mother.

Goodwife Barbara was kneeling in the kitchen garden. Kate breathed in the pungent, heady aroma of
the herbs, and watched for a moment as her mother
dug and pulled and planted. There were parsley,
thyme, sage, and marjoram, used for cooking and
preserving. But there were also wormwood for fever
and headache, lavender for sleeplessness, horehound
for coughs, and scores of plants Kate didn't know by
name or function. Soon Master Clement would teach
her!

Goodwife Barbara looked up and smiled. She
straightened her back. "Are you off to the cobbler's?"

Kate repeated her grimace. "I wish I didn't have
to. Jankin's so mean." She sighed.

"Jankin is certainly rude. As well as greedy. Though he could earn far more coins if he finished his work on time. Do not be surprised if the boots aren't done."

"But why go to him at all?" asked Kate.

"He is a gifted craftsman. There's no one else in the district with half his skill."

"He said awful things to Father last night. And that he'd go into the forest himself to hunt down the dragon. Mother, do you believe the dragon's back?"

"I know not, but I believe such rumors must be taken with seriousness."

"Are you afraid?"

"Afraid?" Goodwife Barbara thought for a moment. "Of course I'm afraid! Only a fool would not be. But I'll keep my reason—unlike others you'll see during the next days." Her voice softened. "It seems only yesterday we were made to stay in that cellar. Though I was far younger than you are now, I've never forgotten."

Kate shivered, for she'd heard the tale many times before.

"Even now when I look at the sky at night I remember the dark shapes flying overhead. And the stench! Never again have I smelled such sickness and corruption." Goodwife Barbara shuddered. "People said the flying shapes were dragons, and that we would all be destroyed in our sleep—especially the young maids of the village."

"Tell me about the cave!"

"You've heard it more times than I can remember," said her mother with a faint smile. "Well, why not?" she added, shrugging with resignation. "As you know, it was a cellar prepared by the men. The women placed food and drink inside. One terrible week some of us spent every night in that hole."

"Was it awful?"

"It was damp and dark. We heard strange noises and rustlings, and we knew not what was happening outside. The dragon never came, but it was dreadful—dreadful!"

"Mother, do you really think the monster devoured all of those hunters?"

"What else? The whole town hunted the length and breadth of the forest. No sign of them was ever found."

"Have you ever wished you could see him?"

"The dragon? No," answered Goodwife Barbara firmly. "I don't need to see the dragon to know he exists. Unlike someone . . ." Her voice trailed off.

"Who, Mother?"

"She used to wonder . . . she said the strangest things . . ."

"What did she say?"

"She wondered if dragons were real!" said Goodwife Barbara in a rush.

Who was this person? thought Kate. Who would have such ideas? "Do I know her?"

"Her name is Rose," said Goodwife Barbara

slowly. "Most people call her Mad Rose. She lives in the forest. Many years ago she was a friend of your Grandmother Kate."

"I've heard of Mad Rose, but I thought she was long dead. Why does no one speak of her?"

"Middlethorpe may have been unjust to her," said Goodwife Barbara thoughtfully. "But I confess I found her odd . . . her ideas made me uncomfortable." She shook her head as if to rid it of unpleasant thoughts, and rose to her feet. "Go now, child. Do your errands. I must see about the dinner." Goodwife Barbara picked up her basket, leaving Kate to set out reluctantly for the shop of Jankin, the cobbler.

It was the weekly market day, and the square teemed with life. As she neared Spice Alley, Kate heard a familiar wheezing and snuffling above the haggling and bargaining of Middlethorpe's housewives. She turned, and directly behind her was Bruin, the wonderful dancing bear who traveled from fair to fair with his master, Simkin, and whom she had glimpsed the day before in her rush to Daisy's merrymaking. Was it possible that less than a day had passed since then?

"Simkin!"

"Hello, little miss. It cheers me to see you. And I venture to say that Bruin is pleased as well." Simkin's leathery brown face was almost lost in the folds of an ancient hood. He peered at her out of its depths with sharp black eyes. As always, Kate wondered where Simkin had learned his elaborately polite speech. But that, like everything else about him, was a mystery.

"Bruin, say hello to the little miss."

Kate touched the extended paw. "How do you do, Bruin? Will you dance for me?"

Simkin clapped his hands sharply and hummed a tune. The big bear revolved slowly. When the tune stopped, so did Bruin.

"Aren't you early for the fair, Simkin?" asked Kate. "Father's just back from Flanders, and things aren't near ready to begin."

"Yes. I am early." Simkin drew closer and whispered. "And now I wonder if there'll even be a fair. There's strange talk on the square, and I heard it already yesterday in Thornleigh." Simkin shook his head with worry as he made to leave, the great bear on a brass chain following him like an obedient child. So Fife wasn't the only one spreading the story! And there were rumors in Thornleigh, just as the peddler had said. Kate's heart felt tight in her chest, and her skin prickled with excitement.

She spied fat Biddy, almost hidden behind a vast mound of plucked chickens and ducks. "What'll you have, dearie? Just look at this fine bird," she called out to Kate, holding up a fat hen for her inspection.

"Nothing today, Biddy, thanks, but where's Toby?" Kate looked around for Biddy's grandson, who usually helped out on market day.

"His mum wanted 'im home to help with the baby chicks," answered Biddy. "And I'm that sorry," she

confided in a lowered voice. "With all o' them rumors, I don't like travelin' home alone this evenin'."
She looked around anxiously. "Have you heard it,
dearie? The talk?"

"You mean about the dragon?"

The old woman leaned over. "They say he's finally
come back, the murderin' brute, and that he's lurkin'
in the forests just outside the town."

"Do you think it's true?"

"It's been the talk of the market all mornin'. They
say folks brought the news from Thornleigh, and
them what comes from the other way had the same
tale to tell." Biddy looked around cautiously. "Somethin' funny goin' on, dearie. I don't know where the
talk begun, but I'm that scared."

Kate let the sound and commotion of the market-
place swirl around her. Now that Simkin and Biddy
had alerted her, she began to notice that something
was different—a tension and strain in people's faces;
clumps of men and women whispering and gesturing. There were none of the usual shrieks and bel-
lows of laughter, no good-natured shouts from one
end of the square to the other, no boisterous happy
noise as on other market days.

Kate wandered among the market stalls, among
the pushing and shoving, the haggling and bargaining, trying to pick out conversations. But she could
make out nothing. Whatever was being said about
the dragon was being said very quietly. Kate recalled
Simkin's and Biddy's whispering. People were afraid.

She gave up and headed for Spice Alley, where both Master Clement and Jankin had their shops. First Jankin, she decided. The worst first.

The large boot that hung above Jankin's door already hinted of the atmosphere inside. Its paint was peeling. One of the thongs had snapped, and the boot hung drab and off-balance. Kate stood still for a moment. Then she took a deep breath, pushed open the door, and entered the long narrow room that impressed her, as always, with its dust, darkness, and clutter. A rough wooden table was heaped with piles of leather, bundles of lacings, half-finished boots and slippers, and a jumble of tools and trimmings. A figure stepped out of the dimness in the rear of the shop. It was Jankin, and Kate felt herself go rigid with dislike. His hair and beard were dirty and unkempt. He wore his usual greasy clothes and tattered leather apron.

"Well, well, well," he said, taking a long swallow from the tankard in his hand. "The daughter of the fancy merchant, I do declare! Miss High and Mighty herself!"

"Call me anything you like." Don't let him know how he frightens you, Kate told herself, staring back defiantly.

"What brings you here, then, Miss Merchant's Daughter?"

"I've come for Father's boots."

"Boots? What boots?"

"The ones he ordered before he went off on his last trip. Aren't they finished yet?"

"No, they're not finished. They're not even begun."

"Jankin, he needs them!"

"For what? To go dragon hunting, maybe?"

Kate held her tongue. She thought of her mother's words about Jankin's skill. There had to be a decent cobbler in the district besides this obnoxious person!

Jankin leaned closer. "What're he and the other burgesses doing about that wicked monster, if I might ask? I take it you've heard the rumors?"

"Of course I've heard! From the person who told you, no doubt! I thought he'd be with you this moment."

"You'll yet be glad of Fife, Miss Haughty Kate. Well," he said, "what're they going to do?"

"I don't know." She stared straight into his eyes without blinking.

"Someone'd better think of going for that monster. Otherwise I might just go hunt 'im down myself. You've heard of the dragon treasure, have you? And of the pearl in his forehead? Maybe Jankin'll get there first and become a rich man. Maybe then I can build myself a fine house like your father." He burst into raucous laughter.

Kate felt her cheeks flame. "How dare you always talk that way about my father! He's done nothing to you!"

"In truth he hasn't. He and those other burgesses. As long as they get their gold, naught else matters. Maybe that's how I'll do things from now on. And that monster may just help me!" He picked up his tankard. "You'd better go." He took a long swallow of ale and, ignoring Kate, headed for the rear of the shop.

Kate watched him, puzzling over his last words. What was Jankin up to? Would he go after the dragon on his own? She stood for a moment thinking. Then she ran out the door and hurried down the street to the welcoming shop of Master Clement.

"Master!"

There was no answer, but the door to the garden was open, and she found Master Clement, like her mother, working among his herbs.

"Ah, my new apprentice has come to assist me!" He looked up and smiled. Kate's heart lifted with excitement and pleasure. "Here, my daughter." Master Clement handed Kate a mixed bundle of plants in which she recognized only some sprigs of lavender and wormwood.

"Oh, Master, I've so much to learn!" exclaimed Kate with a sudden sense of discouragement. "I hardly know any of these by name." She took his extended hand and helped him to his feet.

"Soon you will know the names and functions of them all, as well as many others," the master reassured her, entering the shop. "Here, put them on the counter for now. I'll take care of them later." As usual, he folded his long body onto the tall stool, and motioned Kate to sit on the shallow steps that led to his private living quarters. "How can I serve you?"

"Master, do you think the dragon has returned?"

"I cannot say, my daughter, but yesterday in the forest I sensed evil around me. And, as you know, I do not fear the woods. Still, who can tell? There is at least one person I know who would not agree with me. And the forest is her home."

Was it possible? But it had to be! "Are you speaking of Mad Rose?"

Master Clement looked startled. "Strange you should know her name, for it is rarely heard these days. But yes. I speak of Rose. A strong and wise woman, much abused by the people of Middlethorpe."

"Tell me of her, Master! Mother said she was strange, and that the people of Middlethorpe might have been unjust to her. Why?"

"Many are afraid of Rose. And they feel guilt because she was driven into the forest to live alone— or die."

"I never knew!" Kate was shocked. "I thought she'd been dead for years."

"No. She's not dead. Nor is she mad. It happened soon after the dragon hunt. Her husband was Hick, the plowman, one of the nine who were lost. Some held her responsible."

"Why?"

"People said she was in league with Satan. That she'd set the dragon on the men."

"Why would she do that? With her own husband one of the hunters?" Kate thought of poor Mad Rose, alone in the forest.

"Hick was a man of many disappointments, and

he became cruel and vicious. He beat Rose, and often left her for long periods of time. It was then that I taught her about herbs. I and your Grandmother Kate."

"Why?"

"She needed a skill or she would have starved. And she loved the healing arts."

"Why did others hate her?"

"Rose was outspoken, and she was poor. All her life she'd been independent and cleverer than most. People were afraid of her. They thought she wanted the hunters dead so she'd be free of Hick."

"That's a terrible thing to think."

"Yes. Rose is a good woman who has never harmed anyone. The people of Middlethorpe were mad—not Rose."

"How does she live, Master? And where?"

"Deep in the forest. She eats fruits and berries, and traps small animals for food."

"But why do you say Rose does not believe there is evil in the forest? Because of the dragon, I mean."

"Rose has never feared the dragon."

"How could she not? Dragons are terrible creatures! And she all alone!"

Master Clement looked at the half-open window. He leaned over and whispered, "She does not believe that dragons exist."

"That's what Mother . . ."

"Sh-sh-sh-sh. Say nothing of this, my daughter."

"But Master! How did she . . ."

"My child, lower your voice. I have told you all I know."

"But is that all she said?"

"Just that. We never spoke of it again."

"I want to meet her."

"It could be dangerous for you both."

"Why? Why should it be dangerous?"

"Because Rose has no fear, and her ideas are new. Some think them dangerous. That can cause trouble even for a man, but for a woman . . ."

"Master, why should this be? Why should women and young maids not have ideas of their own?" She looked at the apothecary with dismay. "Do you think that, as well?"

"How could you believe such a thing of me?" Master Clement looked equally distressed. "I love Rose and I love you. In part because of the free spirit I sense in you both. But you see what it's brought her. Banishment and loneliness. My daughter, I don't want that for you!"

"There's something else I want to ask," said Kate. "Master, do you know about unicorns?"

"I do, a little."

"What are they like?"

"They are said to resemble a small horse, with a curling beard and cloven hooves. Their coat is of the purest white. A long slender horn grows out of their forehead and spirals to a point."

"They must be beautiful," breathed Kate.

"Indeed. Though I have never seen one. And very

strong and proud. The unicorn roams the forest alone and seeks no allies."

"Father told me that unicorns cannot be caught except by a young maid in the forest."

"So they say," agreed Master Clement. "And, sadly, some maids have helped to capture unicorns for their precious horn. It is a safeguard against poisons and foulness. Even when powdered, it is worth ten times its weight in gold because of its healing powers. Wait, I will show you."

He disappeared into his private quarters. A moment later he returned with a small box of ivory, richly carved with fruits and flowers, and fitted with a silver clasp.

"Look." The little casket was filled to the rim with a fine white powder. "Truly a magic powder," said Master Clement with reverence.

"It must be worth many bags of gold!"

"That is so. I received it as a gift from a wise and good man. But unscrupulous people have ground up the horns of other animals and sold the powder as that of the unicorn. An evil practice!" He closed the lid of the little casket. "Tell no one you saw this." He smiled. "Now that you are my apprentice, I must share some secrets with you. Secrets of the trade. And soon I shall speak to your father so we may begin our work. Once this dragon matter is resolved."

"I don't know what to say to Father," said Kate, suddenly blurting out her worries. "He can be unreasonable. And Mother scolds me because I'm untidy."

Master Clement laughed. "Do not distress yourself. I'll talk with them both. Between us, we'll surely persuade them."

Reassured and much happier, Kate left the shop, almost colliding with Fife. The peddler was tying his mule to a post with a length of frayed rope.

"Fife, how long have you been here?" she asked, remembering the half-open window with a jolt of anxiety.

"Just this minute. Though why you should care, Miss, is beyond my ken," said the peddler in his usual whining manner, unlike the wild fear he had shown the previous day. He put a final knot into the rope, and shambled into Master Clement's shop.

What if he had heard? What if Fife had crept up and seen the little casket? Once more Kate glanced uneasily at the window. Then, reluctantly, she set out for home.

5

Master Clement Stands Fast

I t had not been a good afternoon. Kate had walked with Geoffrey down to the fields near the village, where he had promised to help build the fires that were to be lit that evening. Then she had gone on to stay with Daisy and little Robin. But Daisy, more and more terrified by the growing rumors, had spent the entire time listening for strange noises, looking at the windswept sky, watching the dark line of the distant forest, waiting for the beast to appear.

"Miss!" she exclaimed, clutching the little boy, "I saw shadows last night, and strange flashes of light, just like Fife. It's the monster! I know it is! Oh, Miss, we're all going to die!"

By the time Rob and Geoffrey returned, the fires had been lit and already clouds of reeking smoke hovered over the meadows.

"You can't imagine how disgusting that stuff is," said Geoffrey. He shuddered. "Rob, how do you bear it?"

"But that's the whole point of it! We have to. We got no other protection."

To Kate's surprise, Rob had insisted on walking with her and Geoffrey as far as the town gate. They hurried along the highroad, careful to avoid ruts and stones in the darkening night.

"Look, the flames!" Kate could see dim shapes moving about from fire to fire. She knew Tim was there somewhere, and prayed he would take care. "It reminds me of Mother's tales," she said with a shiver.

"What tales?" Rob stopped abruptly to face her. "What tales, Miss?"

"When . . . when she was young," stammered Kate, shocked, for she saw fear in his eyes. "One time there were shapes of dragons flying overhead, and the whole village panicked." Involuntarily she looked up. Billowing clouds of smoke, tattered by the wind, were murky against the sky. Her skin prickled and she swallowed hard. "I think I know how she felt."

Rob turned and began to walk faster. "Let's hurry! Who's to know when that dragon'll come flyin' through?"

"What's the matter, Rob?" Geoffrey teased. "You want to go back?"

"I can't," said Rob grimly, offering no explanation, walking more quickly than ever.

Geoffrey and Kate exchanged puzzled glances, and hurried to keep up with him. Kate looked again at the shifting patterns of smoke and cloud. Was it possible . . . her heart stopped . . . could one of those shadows swoop down to destroy them? No! It could not be. And yet . . . Her stomach and chest tightened. She struggled for breath.

"Look." Geoffrey pointed. "Someone's waiting. Out by the gate. It's Jankin!" he exclaimed as they drew closer.

"Ho! Who goes there?" called the man. "Is that Rob, the gatekeeper?"

"It is," muttered Rob.

"What took so long?" demanded Jankin. "You're late."

"Late?" exclaimed Kate.

"We were meetin' at the Goose!" said Rob heatedly. "Why're you out here?"

"We changed it to the square. I came to head you off."

"Rob! Why are you meeting with Jankin?"

"Since when must the gatekeeper ask your permission, Miss Merchant's Daughter?" Jankin turned to go. "Come then, Rob, it's getting late."

Rob shrugged helplessly. "You'll be all right?"

"Of course," replied Kate, puzzled. Why should decent, honest Rob have secret dealings with that cobbler?

"Come, Sister. Let's go." Geoffrey set out in the direction of home, and reluctantly Kate followed. Moments later, when she turned to look, Jankin and Rob had disappeared into the night.

"Brother! There's something strange going on. Let's follow them!" Just being inside the walls of Middlethorpe gave Kate courage.

Geoffrey stared at her for a moment. "You're right. Let's go!"

They hurried along the shadowed streets and arrived at the square out of breath, less from running than excitement. Flattening their bodies against a building, they peered around a corner into the open expanse of cobbles, still faintly touched with light. Two figures stood on the Guildhall steps.

"It's Jankin and Rob," whispered Geoffrey.

"What're they doing?"

"Let's sneak around behind the stocks so we can hear."

They skirted the edge of the square.

"Sister, stay in the shadows. They're bound to see us."

"Listen." Kate clutched his arm.

"Over here, Peddler!" It was Jankin's voice.

"You took long enough!" complained Rob, as the peddler crossed the square to meet them.

"You'll not regret the waiting." Fife's familiar whine was unmistakable.

"Now then, Peddler, what's so important we should meet here this time of night?" asked Jankin.

"I've a strange tale, if it's worth somethin' to you."

"Well," said the cobbler, "tell us."

"A few coins wouldn't hurt at all . . ." Fife's whine made Kate's skin crawl.

"You'll get no coins from me!" Rob turned away violently, and made as if to leave.

"Wait!" said Jankin, holding him back. "He may know something."

"Not a penny from me!" repeated Rob. "I came to talk of protectin' Daisy and Robin, not to throw away my few hard-earned coins."

So that's why Rob was here! Suddenly Kate understood.

"Leave us be," continued Rob. "You've naught to tell us."

"Ah, but I do," said Fife. The irritating whine was gone, and suddenly the peddler seemed to know he had control.

Jankin flung some coins on the ground before him. "Now tell us what you know. Be quick about it."

"One moment, one moment." Fife bent down and picked the coins from between the cobbles. Straightening up, he stored them carefully in his pouch. "Now then, for my news."

He lowered his voice and spoke rapidly, with many gestures. Kate and Geoffrey could not make out a word. Once he pointed toward Spice Alley. Then, abruptly, he turned to leave.

"Where did you hear this?" Jankin spoke roughly.

"No questions," said Fife. "I've told my tale and kept my bargain. What you do now's no business o' mine."

"Wait!" Jankin grabbed his arm.

"Leave me be!"

"You come with us."

"For what?"

"What else?" said Jankin. "We talk to the old herb grinder himself."

"No. Leave Master Clement alone!" exclaimed Rob.

"Don't be a fool," said Jankin. "We go now. The three of us. And once we have the horn, we round up the others and set off tonight."

"Set off?" questioned the peddler. "Set off where?"

"Into the forest, you fool! What think you all this is for? We're going after the dragon!"

"You're mad!" Rob stared at the cobbler.

"Not mad!" replied Jankin. "Clever! And once we get that dragon treasure, I'll be rich as well. And so will you, Gatekeeper!"

"Not me!" said Rob hotly. "I'll be no part o' your dirty work! And I'm not runnin' off on a hunt with you. I'm goin' home to my Daisy." He turned and set off across the square without another word.

Jankin watched him for a moment. Then he shrugged. "Peddler," he said, "if you come with me I promise you won't regret it."

Fife considered, then nodded, and together they set off. As they turned into Spice Alley, Kate gripped her brother's arm.

"Geoffrey, listen." In a rapid whisper she told him what Master Clement had said about the unicorn horn. "That's what the peddler was telling them. I'm sure of it. We've got to follow them."

"Why?" asked Geoffrey. "Why would they want it?"

"It has great healing powers," whispered Kate as they made their way along the edges of the square. "He wants the magic powder for protection."

When they reached the crooked little street they continued to stay in the shadows of the houses. Even before they had reached the bend near Master Clement's shop, they heard a commotion, and when they rounded it they saw Jankin banging on the door.

"Open up, old man! Or we'll break it down."

"He's acting like a brute!"

"Sh-sh-sh, Sister. Don't let them hear you."

The door opened, and light from Master Clement's candle shone faintly in the street. There was some muffled conversation. Then Fife and Jankin walked in and pulled the door shut behind them.

Kate tugged at Geoffrey's arm. "Look up at the sky," she whispered. "Those shadows . . . could it be . . . ?"

"Nothing!" Geoffrey shook off her arm. "Nothing but smoke and clouds." He looked up and down the street. "Where are the neighbors? It's like a graveyard." His hand was on the door.

"Wait," whispered Kate. "Let's see what's happening first."

Without making a sound, Geoffrey managed to open the door a crack so they could look inside.

"We want that powder, old man! That unicorn horn!" Jankin wasn't in Kate's line of vision, but his rough bullying manner was enough to send new anger surging through her.

"What do you mean? What unicorn horn?" She could see Master Clement, straight and tall, his voice controlled and dignified, as always.

"In a pretty little box," said Fife. "A white powder, Master. You should keep your windows closed when you have private business." He gave the apothecary a knowing leer.

Kate nudged Geoffrey. "I knew it! I knew he was listening."

Master Clement looked at the peddler with distaste. "I thought better of you, Fife." He turned to the cobbler. "As for you, Jankin, I'll give you nothing."

"Don't play with us, old man, if you know what's good for you! We need that powder. Now!"

"I'll not be forced into giving any of my medicines away," said Master Clement, "and certainly not to a bunch of ruffians. I'm surprised at you, Jankin," he said, "and you, Fife. Only this morning I gave you herbs for your Peterkin. And tonight you betray me. For coins, I've no doubt."

"Don't answer him, Peddler!" ordered Jankin. "Keep your counsel." He planted himself in front of Master Clement. "Fife, here, tells me wonderful things about this powder of yours. That it has a strange magic. I want it, old man!"

"Why?" asked the apothecary. "Why do you need it?"

"It's naught you need to bother yourself with." Jankin walked restlessly around the shop, fingering jars and bottles, picking up the weights on Master Clement's scales, dropping them carelessly on the counter. "Just give it to us! I'm losing patience, and the hour is late!" Kate held her breath. "Trust us," he added with a burst of raucous laughter.

Master Clement faced him without flinching. "Are you going after the dragon? I need my supply of powdered horn for all the hunters. I cannot share it with men who defy the others and go off on their own."

"Then we'll find it ourselves!" shouted Jankin, flying into a rage. He picked up a large glass bottle and slammed it to the ground. It exploded into shards and splinters that caught the light of Master Clement's candle as they hit the floor and sprayed in all directions.

"Geoffrey! We need to help. Come on!" Kate pushed open the door but almost lost her balance as someone burst through ahead of them and shouldered his way into the shop.

It was Rob! Kate held her breath as he strode across the room and grabbed Jankin. "Are you out of your senses?"

"Leave me alone!" shouted Jankin. "I'm going to find that powder if I have to break every jar in the place." He wrenched himself free from Rob and sent a shelf of bottles crashing and splintering on the floor. "No fool of an addled old man is going to stop me! Nor are you, Gatekeeper!" he added.

Kate ran to Master Clement, who stood helplessly watching, unaware of the candlestick in his hand, aslant and dripping wax. She took it from him and placed it on the counter. "Master."

"Kate! My child!" He looked at her in confusion. "What brings you here?"

"We've come to help, Geoffrey and I." She watched as Rob once again tried to pull Jankin away from the shelves, with Geoffrey ready to help. Fife, she noticed with contempt, had moved into a shadowed corner as far as possible from the fray.

Jankin seemed possessed of a kind of manic strength. He broke away as Rob tried to restrain him, grabbing and slamming down jar after jar. No longer did he even trouble to examine their contents. The destruction seemed all that mattered.

"Peddler!" he shouted, struggling to escape Rob and Geoffrey's hold, "help me!" He lashed out at Rob, sweeping a whole shelf of crockery to the ground. "Get away from me, scum!" The jars hit the stone floor with a crash. As Jankin's arm swung clear of the shelf, Rob grabbed it and twisted it against the cobbler's back.

"Leave me be!" Jankin struggled, but at last Rob's height and bulk were too much for him. "Fife!" he yelled. "For God's sake, man, don't just stand there! Help me!"

But Fife had pushed his way through the curtain that led into Master Clement's private quarters. Kate glanced at Master Clement, who had watched the peddler as if in a trance. Oh, please, she prayed, please, let the box be well hidden, and don't let him find it! After several heart-stopping moments, Fife reappeared without the little casket. At that moment Jankin broke loose from Rob's grip, and brushed past the counter in a rage. He stopped, lifted the heavy stone mortar over his head, and hurled it to the floor. It hit the stones and broke into pieces.

"What've you done?" Rob's voice sent a chill through Kate. It was a voice she had not heard before. "That mortar's cured many a sickness. Only last Eastertide the master ground herbs in it for baby Robin." He made as if to grab Jankin, but the cobbler leaped out of his way and straightened up, ready to attack him. The two men stood, facing each other, their eyes locked. Without a sound. Without movement. At last, Jankin shrugged and turned away. "All right, old man," he said, "you've won. We're leaving." Then before anyone knew what was happening, he grabbed Master Clement by the front of his robe.

Kate watched in horror as he yanked Master Clement toward him, pushed him away hard, and let go. The master stumbled, tripped backward, and fell, hitting his head on a sharp edge of the broken mortar. Then all was quiet. He lay on the stone floor, blood running from a deep slash on his head.

Kate rushed to help him. She found a rag on the counter and tried to stanch the blood that ran down his face. Jankin and Fife watched without a word. For a moment Rob looked stunned. Then with a quick motion he walked to the cobbler and pulled him by the arm. "Get out," he said in that new, chilling voice, "if you know what's good for you. And you, Peddler. Now."

Jankin stood for a moment in Rob's grip. Then, with a sudden movement, he twisted himself free and headed for the door. Fife followed, and Kate, with a shuddering sense of relief, heard the door slam behind them.

For a moment the only sound was Master Clement's tortured and irregular breathing. Kate looked at Geoffrey. "We'd better do something. The master needs care."

"You stay with Rob," said Geoffrey, heading for the door. "I'll get Father. We'll bring the chestnut and take Master Clement home with us."

"It's dangerous out there alone! Those shadows! We don't know what they might be!"

"Someone has to go," said Geoffrey. "I can outrun any dragon," he said, forcing a grin. "And Mother will know what to do for the master."

Kate said no more, stifling her worry as Geoffrey hurried off into the night. She sat down beside the gatekeeper. "Rob, however did you get mixed up with them?"

Suddenly Rob slumped. "Oh, Miss, we were goin' to talk about that monster—and what to do! Daisy is out of her mind with fear—you saw her this afternoon—and so's the whole village! Those fires aren't goin' to stop that dragon, and naught else is bein' done."

"But why Jankin?"

"I'd rather it'd been Master Simon, Miss. But all he said was wait. Anyway, we were just goin' to meet at the Goose and talk. And then the peddler told Jankin to meet 'im in the square. You heard 'im at the gate. Jankin didn't want everyone to come along. Just me. So I went." He roused himself. "What're you doin' here, then? Why aren't you at home?"

"We followed after you left us. We saw you with Fife."

"You saw us? And heard?"

"Just the part where he wanted money. But I know what he told you."

"How could you, if you didn't hear?"

"Rob. I knew it was about the unicorn horn. That's why we followed."

"How'd you know?"

"Master Clement was showing me the little casket this morning when Fife was listening. You heard him just now." She looked at him. "Rob, why did you leave and then come back?"

"I was on my way home to Daisy, but then I realized what Jankin was planning to do. It seemed that the master might need me." He sighed. "In truth, I was right."

"Why does Jankin want the powder?"

Rob brushed a strand of damp hair out of Master Clement's face. "He wants to go after the dragon."

"When do you think he'll go?"

"Right away."

"But why? Why can't he wait?"

"It's the treasure, Miss. He wants to be the first to reach that monster."

Master Clement stirred. He moaned and tried to touch the wound. Gently Rob pulled his hand away and dabbed at the cut, which had stopped trickling blood.

They sat in silence, Rob tending the master's cut.

"Listen!" exclaimed Kate. "I think they're here." As she spoke, the door opened, admitting Geoffrey and her father.

Master Simon stood for a moment, looking at the destruction in the shadowy room, and at the prone and bleeding form of Master Clement.

"It is a madness!" he exclaimed softly to himself. "A madness that has taken hold of us since this dragon rumor began." He walked swiftly across the room, his boots crunching over the fragments of glass that littered the floor. "Come, Geoffrey, Rob. Help me bring him to the chestnut. We must hurry."

As she ran to hold open the door, Kate felt herself go limp with exhaustion and relief. They brought the half-conscious apothecary outside, and together lifted him onto the mare's back. With Geoffrey on the saddle behind him for support, Master Simon leading the chestnut, and Kate and Rob walking on either side, they brought Master Clement through the streets of Middlethorpe. The sky was dark, the brightness of the moon blotted out by clouds. Kate shivered with a kind of dread as they hurried through the streets.

Home at last, they watched while Goodwife Barbara bathed the apothecary's wound, cleansed it with wine, and bandaged it with soft, clean linen. And there on a pallet beside the hearth, in the warmth of the kitchen fire, Master Clement slept fitfully while Kate and her mother watched beside him for the rest of the night.

6

The Hunters Depart

Kate struggled through deep underbrush. A pungent odor sickened her. It was the smell of dragons, said Master Clement, who was in front of her. It was the smell of evil, said Brother Luke, who was behind. A steady pounding made her head ache. "It's the hunters up ahead," said Master Clement. "Your Grandfather John's men. They're killing the dragon, pounding on his tail, his heavy scaly hide—pounding, pounding, pounding."

Kate clapped her hands over her ears to shut out the noise. She ran—toward Grandfather John, whom she'd never known, and toward the dragon. Faster, faster, tripping over roots, running, running, running. She stumbled and fell hard.

And woke up! Great waves of relief swept over her. She was safe at home, not in the terrifying forest! But why was she sitting, her back propped against the cold stone of the hearth? She looked and remembered. For there was Master Clement, tossing restlessly in his sleep, the bandage on his head caked with dried blood. Janet stood at the kitchen table pounding a slab of mutton.

Footsteps sounded in the hall and Master Simon entered the room, followed by Rob. The gatekeeper had gone home the night before to be with Daisy, but had promised to return in the morning.

"Master, I'm ready."

"Then let us be off. I know not what the day may bring, but I'm grateful to have you with me for assistance."

"Father, where are you going?" Kate tried to pull herself out of her dream.

"First to the Guildhall to speak with the burgesses. After that, who knows? We'll see what decisions are made."

"Have you heard?" said Rob. "The cobbler's gone off to the forest. Early this mornin' he came to the village lookin' for men to go with 'im. Said he was tired o' waitin' for the burgesses to make up their minds."

"Why?" exclaimed Master Simon. "Why would he suddenly go after the dragon like that? Jankin's always full of bluster, but this . . . ?"

"He planned it from the start!" Kate broke in. "Don't you see? That's why he wanted the unicorn horn."

"And now he's gone without it," said Master Simon heavily.

"And Fife with 'im," added Rob.

"Who else?" asked Kate.

"The fishmonger," said Rob.

"And the baker!" said Janet, who had stopped pounding the meat so she could listen. "Two of his little ones are sick, an' he says it's the dragon that's to blame."

"And who's to say he's not right?" said Rob. "My Daisy's out o' her mind with worry about our Robin. And I'm startin' to feel the same."

"Old Biddy came round to my mum's with some eggs this mornin'," said Janet. "Her Toby's been taken sick, and the baby chicks are dyin' off one by one. I'm scared, I am! We're all goin' to die. I know we are!"

"No one's going to die," said Geoffrey, who had just come in. "Don't be foolish! Father, if there's a hunt, may I take that polished spear of Grandfather's?"

"Right now there's no way of knowing if there'll be a hunt," replied Master Simon. "And I, for one, hope there won't be."

"Mother gave me this," said Geoffrey, "but it's no use without a bow."

"What is it?" asked Kate. Geoffrey was holding a short wooden rod.

"One of the bolts to Grandfather's crossbow. He took all the others along on the dragon hunt."

"It's beautiful," said Kate, examining its curious inlay of ebony and silver.

"Come, Rob," said Master Simon. "Let's be on our

way. The burgesses are gathering this very moment."

"If there's a hunt, Father will lead it," whispered Geoffrey to Kate. "You wait! He knows more of the forest than anyone."

"Come with us, my son." Master Simon beckoned to Geoffrey. "Come with Rob and me. You can be of use to us." They turned to leave the room, Geoffrey following.

"Wait, Brother!" Kate grabbed him by the arm. "What about me?"

"You?"

"If there's a hunt. You promised to help."

"Sister! You can't go! I was just teasing."

"You have to help me!"

"How?"

"I need some clothes, and an animal to ride."

Geoffrey studied her for a moment. "You really mean it, don't you? You really mean to go."

"Of course I do!"

"Father won't let you."

"I'm not asking him!"

Geoffrey stared at her. "He'll find out, Sister, and stop you."

Kate stared back. "Will you help me or not?"

Geoffrey shrugged. "If they really decide on a hunt, I'll try to find you a horse." He headed for the door.

"What about clothes?"

"Look in my chest. Something in there should fit. I'll see you in the square." He was gone.

Kate hurried upstairs. Rummaging through Geoffrey's clothes chest, she found tights, a tunic, and a hood that covered the shoulders. If she pulled it down far enough, wrapped the long liripipe high around her neck and chin, she might not be recognized. There were even shoes of soft leather that would fit if she stuffed the toes with grass or rags. Maybe, just maybe, with good fortune and Geoffrey's help, she would get out of Middlethorpe unnoticed!

As she closed the chest its heavy lid slipped from her grasp and fell shut with a crash. Kate jumped. Surely her mother would hear! But she was in luck, for Janet was washing pots and making a terrible racket. She stopped for a moment to think. What to do with the clothes till she needed them? Should she put them on now under her dress? No. She would surely be noticed. Besides, no one knew what would happen this morning, what the burgesses would decide. Perhaps she should hide them under her mattress and come back later. No again, for she knew her mother too well. She'd never get out of the house unnoticed. Suddenly she had the answer. Roll them up in a tight bundle and take them along. If needed, she'd find somewhere to change.

It was done! The bundle looked bland, of no interest, and would not raise a single question. Now down the stairs, past the kitchen, and outside. Through the garden and out the gate!

Some villagers were making their way up the street, carrying pikestaffs, flails, crossbows, even shovels and picks. Already word was out that there might be a dragon hunt, and people were prepared for what could happen. Suddenly she spied Tim. Like herself and the peasants, he was headed for the market square.

"Tim! What brings you?" Kate waited for him to catch up, giddy with her good fortune. That he should be passing at just this moment!

"My master wants to know what will happen." Tim fell into step, adjusting his long stride to hers. "But one of the vats is bubbling with molten glass, ready for the adding of color, and he cannot leave it. So he sent me."

"If there's a hunt, will you go?"

"The master said I might, but he's not happy about it."

"I'm going!" Kate burst out before she could stop herself.

"You, Kate?" He stared at her. "Surely you jest!"

"Why?" She bristled. Not Tim, too!

"But . . . but you're a maid!" Tim looked confused and embarrassed. "And there'd be danger!"

"I know," she said soberly. "But not for me alone. What does anyone know about dragons?"

"But . . . why? Why would you go?"

"I'm not certain," said Kate slowly. "I confess that I'm frightened. Of that monster. And of the forest." She thought for a moment. "But I've always wanted to see the dragon of Middlethorpe. Since I was a little girl. And perhaps I could even be of use."

"But what would you do?" Tim was asking seriously, not in jest.

"Maybe I can help if someone gets sick—or wounded. I know a little about healing, and . . . Tim, what if the dragon really hurts someone?"

"Who knows?" Tim looked at her strangely. "Perhaps you're right about coming." He touched her arm. "You're like no other maid I've known."

Kate looked at him. "Tim?"

"Yes?"

"Thank you for not laughing."

Tim's face turned red. "I'd never make fun of you," he said, rumpling his hair furiously.

As they drew near the square they could hear the noise and confusion of people gathering near the Guildhall. People milled around talking and gesturing, clamoring for the burgesses. "What's happenin'?" asked an enormous woman carrying a market basket. "Only yesterday the news was the burgesses'd do nothin' 'cause they thought it'd hurt the fair."

"It started with the cobbler," replied her companion, a tired-looking woman with three small children clinging to her skirts. "He went and beat Master Clement last night. An' then he went off in the woods after the monster."

"Why ever would Jankin beat the apothecary?" wondered the fat woman. "And why set off into the forest like that?"

"I don't know," said the tired-looking woman, whom Kate recognized as the fishmonger's wife.

"But my man went with 'im. He was tired o' waitin' for those burgesses to make up their minds."

Kate and Tim stationed themselves on the edge of the crowd, not far from the Guildhall, beside a small boy with a frisky black dog.

"They went in a little while ago," said the boy. "All o' them important folks. Said they'd come out soon's they decided about that hunt."

"You think there'll be a hunt?" asked Tim.

"For sure! Wish I was big enough to go. I'd kill that monster quick and cut out his heart!"

"Whatever for?" asked Kate, surprised at the little boy's bloodthirstiness.

"Well, Miss, I heard tell if you eat of a dragon's heart, you c'n speak the language of animals. Then I could talk with old Blackthorn, here." He fondled the little dog's ears, and Blackthorn yipped and jumped up at him. "I wonder if it's true," he said anxiously. "Blackthorn's my very best friend."

"I've heard the same," said a voice beside them. "And I've often wondered what it would mean to speak with our animals." He patted the mule beside him. "To know what this good friend is thinking."

"Brother Luke!" exclaimed Kate. "What brings you here?"

The little boy was stroking the friar's mule.

"If I am asked to go I shall be ready," replied the friar.

"But why?" insisted Kate. "Surely you don't want to do battle with the monster!"

"My child, if things go badly, there should be a man of God with the hunters. And only our Lord in heaven knows what would be the outcome of such a venture." He turned away for a moment to talk with the boy and play with the yipping Blackthorn.

Kate nudged Tim. "Let's sneak inside," she whispered, pointing to the Guildhall.

"Why?"

"I know a place where there's a tiny hole, so we can see—and maybe hear. And it's right in the chamber where all the glass is."

Tim's eyes sparkled. Any opportunity to look at the exhibits of the Glassblowers' Guild, and to see the colored windows from the inside, was too much to resist.

"Let's hurry. Or they'll come out before we get there." Kate grabbed his hand, and together they wormed their way past the edge of the crowd and around the rear of the Guildhall. They entered through a door that led into a small chamber next to the two large rooms on the ground floor: the large hall for gatherings of the entire guild, and a smaller adjoining one where the burgesses met.

As they entered the small dark room, they could hear the murmur of voices, but nothing distinct. "Over here," whispered Kate. She opened the large, heavy door just far enough for them to squeeze through, and suddenly they stood in a glory of color—pools of red and blue splashed on the vast stone floor by the sun as it poured through the intricate stained glass of the tall, pointed windows that faced the market square.

"I've never seen them this time of day," gasped Tim. "I didn't know . . . they could be this beautiful." He stood rooted to the spot, while Kate hurried across the hall to the door that led to the anteroom where the burgesses were still meeting.

"Come," she whispered. "Here. Here's the crack. We can see. And maybe we can hear a little. We'll take turns."

Tim pulled himself away from the windows, and stopped to admire the ornately wrought beakers that lined the walls. Someday his masterwork would be displayed on these very shelves!

"Hurry! They're talking about Father! Here, you can look!" Tim pressed his face against the crack.

"Can you hear?"

"Your father's saying they have to make a decision. Here, you look. He's your father, after all."

Kate pressed her eye against the crack. "Harry's talking. He's worried about Jankin having gone off into the forest like that."

"I don't blame him," said Tim. "Kate, what's that large weaving on yonder wall?"

Kate answered without looking. "It's a tapestry Lord Hugo gave to the Merchants' Guild. Don't you think it looks like the meadow?"

"It's beautiful!"

"Tim, listen." Kate pulled his face down near the crack. "They're saying Father should lead the hunt.

I knew it! He doesn't look very happy about it, but he knew it was coming." Reluctantly she moved away from the crack. "Your turn."

"They're asking what about the fair," reported Tim. "That your father's always taken the lead. Well," said Tim, "maybe they'll have to do some work for a change." He grinned. "Someone's saying what's the point of preparing for the fair if no one's going to come because they're scared." He put his eye where his ear had been. "That was Harry. Good old Harry, he'll always say everything straight out."

"Let me," said Kate, and Tim moved away from the crack. "They're asking should they tell Lord Hugo." Suddenly she giggled. "Father says absolutely not. That the burgesses are quite able to make their own decisions. Good for you, Father." She clapped her hands silently and did a little dance.

"Listen to them! They're applauding!" Tim had moved to the crack. "And guess what! Quick. Look!" He relinquished his spot. "They're asking your father again. To lead the hunt."

"He's shrugging his shoulders . . . he's throwing up his hands . . . and . . ." Kate laughed. "He's grinning. Could you hear what they said?"

"No."

"Probably something about his wisdom and good judgment. That always makes him blush. Look, they're coming out!"

They raced across the hall and barely made it through the door to the rear chamber when the first of the burgesses entered the room they had just left. "Quick! Around the front. They're going outside!"

Just as they skirted the corner of the Guildhall, the mayor appeared on the front steps, followed by Master Simon and the other burgesses. The crowd roared. The mayor raised his arms for silence. "Citizens! The burgesses have met and decided. There will be a dragon hunt!"

There were loud cheers.

The mayor called for silence. "Master Simon, the wool merchant, has agreed to be the leader." Once again the cheering broke out. Kate cheered too, filled with pride for her father. "The hunters will depart at noon," continued the mayor. "Before then, they will need to ready themselves, their weapons, and their mounts. You, citizens, may help by bringing them provisions for their journey: breads and pies, meat and drink. Give your bundles of food to the brave men who are going out to do battle for us. And now," he concluded, "may the Virgin and St. Christopher be with our hunters and lead them to the dragon, that he may be destroyed and we be safe in our homes once more. That is all, citizens."

"I have to hurry back to my master," said Tim, "and get a horse. He's already said I could take one of his."

"I have things to do as well, before we leave."

"We? What do you mean?"

"You forget. I'm coming, too."

"I've never known a maid like you!" Tim shook his head in disbelief. "I'll see you later, then," he said with a wave, and disappeared into the excited crowd.

Kate looked around the square until she spied Geoffrey standing near the stocks. She hurried over. "Have you a horse for me?"

"This morning Father said I could ride the chestnut if there were a hunt, and I haven't talked with him since."

"Then I'll have to ride behind you on the chestnut."

"Are you mad?"

"No one will know me in your clothes."

"We'll never get away with it. Father will recognize you in a flash."

"Just wait! You won't even know me!" Kate wished she were as confident as she sounded.

"It won't work, Sister. You're mad to think it will."

"You're afraid! And you promised to help!" Kate almost choked, she was so angry.

"I'm not afraid!" Geoffrey's eyes blazed.

"Then prove it, and help instead of hindering me!"

"What if you get caught?"

"Don't worry. You'll still get to go." Kate spoke bitterly. "You have nothing to lose. You're not a maid, after all."

Geoffrey hesitated. He looked ashamed. "Well, all right. But it's still mad."

"I'll see you, then. Later. When we're ready to leave. Don't fail me," she whispered as he left. "I'll never forgive you!"

Kate hurried to the rear of the Guildhall and let herself in through the door she and Tim had taken earlier. The little chamber was deserted. She stopped for a moment and could hear her heart pounding in the dusty silence. Her chest felt tight, and she could scarcely breathe. Her fingers would not do her bidding as she struggled to untie the bundle of clothes. She slipped out of her gown and pulled on Geoffrey's hose and tunic. How free she felt without layers of skirts and petticoats! She jumped up and down, bent her legs at the knees, tried to run. It was wonderful!

Quickly she pulled the green hood over her head and wrapped the liripipe around her neck like a shawl. The day was too warm, but she dared not leave her face completely uncovered. Even in these things she might be recognized, her bravado to Geoffrey notwithstanding. She rolled up her discarded clothes and hid them in a corner. Finally she pulled on Geoffrey's shoes. How strange she felt! And how light on her feet! She hoped she looked like just another town boy. Tucking the last curly strand of hair into the hood, she set out into the square.

It was amazing, thought Kate, that in the midst of all the fear, a festive mood seemed to prevail. Why, with the dangerous hunt, and fear of the terrible monster hanging like a black cloud over the town, were people giddy and full of laughter? But clearly, everyone was in a state of wild excitement. Right now even Kate was much too anxious about the suc-

cess of her plan to give much thought to the reason
for all the upheaval.

Although it was still early, the hunters were as-
sembling, brandishing pikestaffs and lances, spears
and pitchforks for the benefit of cheering onlookers.
There were even some elegant crossbows, inlaid with
silver and precious stones. Some of the guildsmen
wore ornate liveries, but most of the hunters were
simply dressed in tunics and hoods like Kate's. A
number of sleek greyhounds and several fierce-look-
ing mastiffs ran about, wearing heavy collars with
long iron spikes as protection against wolves and
boar.

At last some stablemen came with a dozen or more
packhorses, which were distributed among those
who had no mounts of their own. She spied Geoffrey
on the chestnut, and her father on his favorite black
mare. Why didn't Master Simon go off and take care
of his job as leader? Kate thought she would die of
impatience. But finally he was called away, and she
could see Geoffrey looking for her.

"Over here," she called softly when he was close
enough to hear.

For a moment he looked straight at her, puzzled,
then started to laugh. "You know," he said, "you
may just get away with it. I scarcely recognized you.
Stay here and I'll come back when Father's too busy
to worry about me. And watch out for Mother! She's
coming to bid us farewell."

Geoffrey left, and Kate waited in the shadow of

the Cathedral. She was struck again by the festive mood in the square. Janet giggled and laughed with Davy, the baker's assistant, who was armed with an enormous pitchfork. Rob stood nearby, wearing his usual clothes of rough wool. Harry, the innkeeper, carried a longbow, his quiver of arrows slung over one shoulder. A brown-and-white horse entered the square far on the other side, bearing a familiar figure. It was Tim. He'd made it in time! At that moment a bell began to peal.

The mayor climbed the Guildhall steps, and when the bell's last clang had died away, he motioned for silence. "The moment has come," he said in a ringing voice. "Our hearts go with you, good hunters, as you depart to rid us of this menace, this wicked, vicious dragon that threatens the peace and safety of our town and village. We look to the moment when you return to our midst, bearing the evil heart of the monster. Go, then! May our Lord and the Virgin go with you. Farewell!"

Kate looked up to see the chestnut almost beside her. Geoffrey had been good as his word! Although he reached down to help her, she could have leaped into the saddle, buoyed with elation. Seated behind him, she could not believe she was there, safely mounted and ready to go with the hunters. Triumph almost choked her. And then she heard it. That all-too-familiar voice.

"Geoffrey! My son! I came to bid you farewell." It was their mother.

Kate's elation turned into leaden despair. But she kept her face hidden and did not move a muscle.

"Look what I've brought you."

"Oh, Mother!" Geoffrey gasped with delight. "The spear!"

Kate caught a glimpse of the beautiful polished spear as Goodwife Barbara handed it to Geoffrey. "I could not bear to give you such a fearsome weapon, but your father persuaded me. Who rides with you?" she asked, glancing up at Kate. "Who are you, boy?"

"He's from the other side of the village, Mother, and has no horse."

Goodwife Barbara peered up at the unfamiliar rider. "I know every boy for miles around, but not this one. Why is his face swaddled as though he were braving a winter storm? Come down, boy. Surely we can find another animal for you to ride."

"We can't," said Geoffrey. "We've already tried."

"I will not have you exposed to more danger than necessary," replied Goodwife Barbara. "It is not good that two of you should ride on one beast in such a dangerous undertaking." She looked out over the square. "I wish I could find your father. Surely he'd not approve of this."

"Mother, please, don't!" pleaded Geoffrey.

Kate said nothing, praying that she might disappear into the depths of her hood.

Goodwife Barbara lost patience at last. "Who are you, boy, that you should cause so much trouble?" She stepped close to the chestnut and looked up. "Let me see your face this instant!" She pulled sharply at the lappet of Kate's hood.

"No!" she exclaimed weakly as the hood fell open. "Surely I'm dreaming!"

Kate also hoped this was a nightmare, and that she would wake at any moment. Suddenly, hot with humiliation, she noticed that the hunters were watching. And laughing.

"My own daughter! Dressed like a street urchin! And deceiving us. And you, Geoffrey, helping with this folly! Come down, Kate. This instant!"

It was over. Kate slid off the chestnut and stood, miserable and defeated, beside her mother. Goodwife Barbara's outrage washed over her wave upon wave. But it did not matter anymore. She'd been caught! Hot tears rolled down her cheeks and into the collar of her hood. She could hear the laughter all around but refused to look up. If only the ground would open so she could vanish!

Suddenly a horn shrilled across the square. Other horns took up the call, and the hunters formed a long line, two abreast, for their ride through the narrow streets to the town gates. "I'm sorry, Sister." Geoffrey reached down and touched her arm. "At first I didn't want to help, but now I'm truly sorry. I really tried!"

Kate could only nod, eyes on the ground. Geoffrey touched the chestnut's side, and off they went to join the others, the mare's hooves striking sparks against the cobbles. Minstrels, jugglers, and acrobats hurried to the head of the line, running, leaping, spinning cartwheels, and clearing the way. The hunters were followed by townspeople and peasants, and cheered on by citizens leaning out of top windows as the procession passed beneath them.

As Kate raised her eyes, a brown-and-white horse broke out of the line and rode back across the square. Tim! He was coming toward her! Hastily she brushed the tears from her cheeks.

"Kate!" Tim reined his horse and looked down at her, carefully avoiding the eyes of Goodwife Barbara. "Farewell," he said lamely. For a moment he stayed there, blushing furiously, rumpling his hair as if willing it to take some action. But even though her mother's presence prevented further words, Kate felt better. With a wave of farewell, Tim turned and rode off with a clatter to join the others.

Standing beside her mother, she watched the last riders leave the square. The hunt was on. The bells of Middlethorpe pealed as if to give warning to the beast lurking in the forests and caves beyond. The hunters were on their way. And she, Kate, was not among them!

7

Kate Makes a Decision

It was a time of waiting. A day went by. At home Kate was in disgrace. "I am stunned at your trickery," said Goodwife Barbara again and again, shaking her head in disbelief.

"But Mother," began Kate, and stopped. For how could she explain? That she hadn't asked permission because she knew it would be denied? The situation was hopeless, and Kate knew she would have to endure her mother's bitter words for as long as they might last.

Meanwhile, it was her task to nurse Master Clement—to do whatever she could for his comfort and well-being. Ordinarily this would have given her pleasure. But now? When the hunters were out in the forest? When she wanted more than anything to be there with Tim and Geoffrey and all the rest?

"What do you think is happening?" she asked Master Clement as she brought him a strengthening cup of spiced wine.

"I wish I could say I am not worried," replied the master, sitting up in the ornately carved wall bed. "If only . . ." He sighed and shook his bandaged head.

"If only what?" Kate handed him the silver cup and adjusted his cushions.

"The casket of unicorn horn. If only I had given it to your father."

"But Master! You were tossing with fever!"

"I know, I know. But it angers me nonetheless. What better place for the magical powder than with the hunters? Who knows what may yet befall them?" He drained the cup absentmindedly. "At least the casket is safe," he said, "and for that I am more grateful to you than I can say."

At Master Clement's instruction, Kate had visited his shop and lifted a loose stone in the floor of his private quarters. There, in a niche under the stone, was the precious casket. Now it was hidden under Kate's coverlet, together with the dragon parchment.

Master Clement's eyes had fallen shut, and soon he slept. The house was silent, and Kate felt both bored and anxious. Goodwife Barbara was in the Guildhall with the other women, busy with preparations for the fair. Already tents were springing up on the big meadow outside the town gates. The burgesses hoped that the moment the hunters returned the fair could begin.

It was strange, thought Kate. For with the hunters' departure, all signs of the dragon had ceased. No more sick babies, no missing children, no dying sheep or burning cottages. There was something eerie about it—as though the moment Middlethorpe had decided to challenge him, the monster had disappeared. And yet, in some ways, the fear was greater than ever. Kate, at least, was more frightened than before. Perhaps it was the unfamiliar silence in the town, with so many of the men gone, and everyone sick with worry. And the awful knowledge that if the dragon chose to descend on Middlethorpe, the town would be at his mercy. Perhaps worst of all was the knowledge that they could do nothing. Nothing except wait.

At night the stink fires lit up the fields between Middlethorpe and the forest. The previous night, when the wind had been in their direction, the stench had reached all the way into the streets of the town, and people had muffled their noses with hoods and shawls.

Kate found the silence in the house stifling. Why not go to the market square while Master Clement slept? Perhaps there would be news. Janet promised to keep an eye on the apothecary, and Kate set off, walking listlessly through the hot and muggy streets. When she neared the square her depression lessened, for there was music and singing, and the sound of laughter. Jugglers and mimes and people on stilts were all trying to earn some coins before the formal opening of the fair. Simkin and his bear had been first, but entertainers continued to arrive, undeterred by the dragon rumors. The townspeople came to see

them and be entertained, to push aside for even a
moment the terrible dragging fear of unknown horrors.

Kate listened to the hurdy-gurdy man as he ground
out the same wheezy tunes he had played as long as
she could remember. A fat and pompous guildsman
was being followed by a mime who imitated him
perfectly, to the delight of the onlookers. A juggler
kept half a dozen plates suspended in midair, and
two small dogs jumped through a series of green
hoops. Across the square there were shouts of laughter, and when Kate went to investigate, she found a
minstrel, brilliant in purple and blue, waving his
arms about.

"Yes, indeed," he shouted to the onlookers. "You
need not scoff. I shall do what I said, and tell you a
happy tale about dragons."

"You told us that last time," said the heavy
woman whom Kate had seen the day before. She was
trying to comfort the tired-looking wife of the fishmonger. "An' look what you've done. You've made
my friend weep. And her man out huntin' down that
monster! You ought to be ashamed!"

"Please, goodwives," pleaded the minstrel, "give
us another chance. We'll not disappoint you."

"It's our penny you're after, I know," she grum-
bled, after consulting the fishmonger's wife. "But,
all right, we'll stay. Nothin' sad, mind you! My friend
needs cheerin'."

"I thank you, Goodwife," said the minstrel, readying a large wooden chest. "Good folk," he announced with a sweeping bow, "we are ready to begin. I," he said, pointing to himself, "shall play St. Patrick, that venerable missionary to the people of Ireland. My colleague," he continued, pointing to the minstrel at his side, "will be a large and wily serpent."

Kate pushed and shoved with the rest to get a better look.

St. Patrick faced the serpent. "And now, you loathsome beast, it is your turn. Every other serpent has obeyed my command and jumped into the sea. Now you. And then this lush, green land will be free of your kind forever."

"I will not leave," replied the serpent. "You may have succeeded with the others, but you'll not get rid of me." He stood rooted to the spot, arms folded across his chest, chin stuck out defiantly.

St. Patrick faced him firmly but without anger, as befitted his station. "Say no more, but jump," he ordered. The serpent refused to budge.

"How dare you, slime of the earth! Get out of my sight!" exclaimed St. Patrick, kicking the serpent-minstrel in the shins. The serpent-minstrel responded by lying down on the ground and arranging his body in a snakelike curve. Then he cushioned his head on his arms, closed his eyes, and began to snore loudly.

The audience burst into applause. Kate was enthralled. The fishmonger's wife and her friend hung on the minstrels' every word.

"Serpent," said St. Patrick, recovering his temper. "If you will not leap into the sea, why not take a nap in my chest, instead of lying on that cold, hard ground. Look," he said, pulling out the corner of a large cushion. "You will be warm and cozy."

"The chest is far too small," replied the serpent-minstrel, stretching out his limbs.

"Surely not! Do just try it."

"It is too small," insisted the serpent.

"Truly, I do believe you are wrong."

"I will prove it to you!" exclaimed the serpent crossly. "It is far too small for a serpent as large and magnificent as I." With this, the serpent-minstrel started climbing into the chest. As soon as one leg was in, the St. Patrick–minstrel grabbed the other leg, dumped the serpent-minstrel into the chest, and clapped the lid shut. The onlookers went wild.

"And now, good folk, this serpent shall enter the sea to join the others." St. Patrick gave the chest a mighty shove, and there was a loud groan from inside. "It is done, and I, St. Patrick, have rid the land of a terrible menace!" He bowed low to loud cheering and applause. Even the fishmonger's wife was smiling. "So you see, good people of Middlethorpe, all dragon tales need not end badly. We wish you success with yours."

The serpent-minstrel leaped out of the chest, and the two made their way through the audience, holding out their hoods. The laughing citizens, grateful for a moment of lightheartedness in the midst of their fear, were generous with their pennies.

Kate dropped a coin into the minstrel's hat, suddenly thoughtful, remembering his last words: "All dragon tales need not end badly." It was as though something was nagging at her consciousness, but she did not know what. She wandered across the square, watching the jugglers, and then again the jumping dogs, when it came to her! An idea so simple she could not believe it had taken her so long to think of it. But, simple and right though it seemed, it was also frightening.

Kate started to run, stopped, and made herself walk slowly and sedately across the square and through the streets toward home. Calm and good planning were most important now. She needed to behave as though everything were just as usual. But everything was not! Everything was incredibly strange, for she was about to do the most daring thing she had ever done in her life. And the most important. Surely the most frightening! If only she were strong and clever enough. For Kate had made a decision. It had burst upon her full-blown, and seemed the answer to everything. She, Kate, would go into the forest and take the unicorn horn to the dragon hunters of Middlethorpe!

— 8 —

Alone in the Forest

Once Kate had made her decision, each task seemed to follow the other, simply and in order. She walked home, stunned by the perfection of her plan. For here, at one stroke, the hunters would get their precious unicorn horn and she, Kate, would get to join the hunters after all, and see the dragon!

She rushed upstairs to look once more at the silken powder. Rummaging in Geoffrey's chest, she pulled out his clothes. Later that night, she stole down to the pantry and found several meat pies to take along. But as she invaded her mother's food stores, there was the nagging tug of guilt she had tried to ignore. Deserting her mother during this terror-fraught time was bad enough. But leaving without any word was cruel. Should she tell Master Clement? But no. The master was still too weak for such a burden.

She tiptoed back to her chamber and packed the meat pies into a pouch she had taken from Geoffrey's chest. Then she crept into bed and tried to think of

a solution. Just when she thought there was no answer, it came to her. Daisy! She would stop at Daisy's
on her way to the forest. She would tell her of the
plan and swear her to silence until a full day had
passed. She would make Daisy promise to take Robin
and visit Goodwife Barbara on the following day,
deliver Kate's message, then stay with her until the
hunters' return. Her mother would not, reflected
Kate with a nervous shudder, need to wonder
whether her willful daughter had been carried off by
the dreaded serpent!

Early, early the next morning she crept out of the
house and hurried to Daisy in the village. Though
horrified and tearful at first, Daisy had promised to
deliver the messsage. Kate knew that she was re-
lieved to be staying inside the solid walls of Middlethorpe, and that her mother would be glad of
Daisy's company and that of little Robin.

And now Kate was hurrying through the fields.
The forest loomed larger and larger, trees assuming
individual shapes, the single, dark line of the woods
dissolving into uneven masses. Kate's chest tightened; her heart began to pound. The meadow was
green, gold, and silent, its usual perfection marred
by wisps of smoke from last night's fires, and occasional blackened mounds that reeked of burning
offal. The air was oppressive, and the sun shone fitfully through a thin layer of cloud. There was hardly
a sound save the whisper of grasses as she brushed
through, and the occasional chirp of an insect.

The forest looked cool and inviting, but to Kate it suggested evil. What was it Master Clement had said soon after the rumors began? That he had sensed evil in the forest? The evil of the dragon? Suddenly it hit her with full force. She was doing the unthinkable. She was breaking the unbreakable rule for young maids from Middlethorpe: never, never go into the forest! And she was doing it alone!

How could she even think of finding the hunters in that vast expanse of woods and hidden clearings? What if she lost Master Clement's unicorn casket, or was robbed? She knew that the forest sheltered boar and wolves and other beasts. Perhaps bandits and robbers hid in these wild places. Many a tale was told of their attacks on innocent wayfarers who had taken a shortcut through the woods. And far on the other side in the dreaded caves, was that where the monster lurked? Or had he come out, perhaps hiding just beyond the fringe of trees? Ready to pounce! Who was she, an inexperienced young maid, to fly in the face of all she had ever heard, to ignore every warning she had ever received? And at a time more fearsome than any she had ever known?

Kate felt suddenly limp and helpless, as an overwhelming wave of terror washed over her. Desperately she fought for her bearings and good sense. The hunters might be ill or lost. Her father and Geoffrey might be wounded, even dead! And Tim! Her heart froze. Nothing must happen to Tim! Master Clement had said the substance in the casket was a healing, magic powder. And how else would she ever lay eyes on the dragon? The creature of her precious parchment? The Virgin would surely help; and St. Christopher, friend of all travelers. Together they would lead her to the hunters.

She had reached the first fringe of trees, and could see the trampled weeds and broken branches where the hunters had entered the forest. Kate took a deep breath, gripped the little casket tightly for good luck, and plunged in.

The sunny fields had been silent, but this was something different. It was a stillness, a breathlessness, a waiting. There was no breeze, but the air was cool. The sun filtered through the leaves of ancient beeches and oaks. There was a rich pungent smell of earth, of wet decaying leaves, of green growing things. Kate could still see the sunlit meadow, but to her surprise she felt no terror in the woods. These saplings and shrubs, these patches of shadow and sun, even the towering oak and beech trees did not resemble the frightening images she had absorbed through countless tales. This forest was not dark, or cold, or filled with evil sounds and smells.

But soon the relief she had felt only moments before vanished. The woods were endless, the dragon caves far on the other side. Though she had never been in the forest, she knew that hunters left markings on trees, or lopped off branches to guide them. And already she saw dung from the horses and mules. But she knew full well that her journey could be long and dangerous. Even if there were no wolves or robbers, she might get lost and die in this vast and silent place, and no one would ever find her. What madness to have come alone! Desperately she clutched the casket of unicorn horn. Just holding it gave her a mysterious sense of strength and courage, and reminded her why she was here. She put it back into her pouch and walked faster. Time was passing!

She followed the traces left by the hunters straight through the forest toward the caves, where the dragon was said to have his lair. As she made her way through saplings and shrubbery, she munched a meat pie. She was thirsty, and had brought no water, so she chewed leaves to moisten her dry throat. In this part of the woods the trees were not so tall, and there were dense thickets of gorse and blackthorn. Blackthorn. She smiled at the memory of the little dog on the square. As she worked her way through heavy undergrowth she realized that had she been dressed in her usual long skirts, she would never have made it. And with the thought, she stumbled and fell. To her astonishment, she was looking directly into the eyes of a doe.

The terrified creature trembled and strained against some bond. As Kate struggled to sit up, she saw that she had tripped over a stout rope well hidden by the underbrush, looped on one end around the forelegs of the little deer. A poacher's trap! And in Lord Hugo's woods! She knew that some poor peasant was depending on that trap to feed his family, and stopped for a moment to consider. Then, unable to leave the doe to her certain death, Kate reached over and slipped off the noose. The terrified creature struggled to her feet and was gone with a bound. Kate felt she had lost a friend in this strange and lonely place.

A moment later the doe reappeared, this time not alone, but with two white-spotted fawns. In a flash, all three made for the deeper forest, and Kate followed, all else forgotten. Twice she thought she had lost them. When she caught up, they were drinking peacefully from a small pool hidden in the trees. They finished, the doe regarded Kate as if to thank her, and in an instant they were gone. This time Kate did not try to follow. She, too, drank from the clear forest pool, and bathed her face. When at last she was ready to continue she stopped, frozen with dismay. She had no idea where she was, and the afternoon was drawing to a close. Kate's self-control cracked. She crumpled into a miserable heap and wept.

Gradually the shadows deepened and the light began to fade. Soon wild beasts would come out to look for food. Soon ghosts and evil spirits would emerge. Soon, for all she knew, the terrible dragon, jaws aflame, would prowl the night forest looking for prey to crush between rows of knife-sharp teeth. Kate huddled on a bed of feathery moss, close to panic, shivering with fear and the sudden chill of the night. She ate her last meat pie, and tried to think what she could do. But her head was muddled with terror and exhaustion. She stumbled through a prayer to the Virgin, adding a special plea to St. Christopher, protector of travelers. Then she squeezed her eyes tightly shut and burrowed into the thick fragrant moss, certain she would not sleep a wink during the whole endless night. But even as she prepared for a dangerous and lonely watch, Kate felt herself drifting off to sleep.

9

Mad Rose

The morning was oppressive. Kate sensed it even before opening her eyes. She stretched her stiff body and slapped at several ants. Her clothes were sticky and scratchy with thorns and brambles. She knew immediately where she was—in the forest, looking for the hunters. But there was something else, something that teased at her, something she dimly felt was wrong but couldn't grasp with her sleep-drugged mind. Then she remembered! She was lost. Lost and alone in this immense and dangerous forest.

Kate sat up with a jolt, now fully awake, and looked around, trying to get her bearings, looking for some trace of the hunters. Any sign that would give her a sense of direction—a sense that they had passed through this part of the forest. She looked for a broken branch, trampled weeds, animal dung, or even a notch carved in a tree. But there was nothing, and as she washed, and drank water to appease her growling stomach, she struggled against a rising sense of panic. It was then she saw the woman sitting on a log, watching her. How long had the woman been there? What did she want? And who was she? But Kate knew. It could be none other than Mad Rose!

The woman was not young. Her skin was toughened by the weather, and her hair was white. She seemed strong and full of energy. Her hair was astonishing, thought Kate. It seemed to have a life of its own. It hung or rather exploded around her shoulders. Kate had never seen such hair. Certainly never on a grown woman. The matrons of Middlethorpe wore kerchiefs to conceal their hair. Even Daisy hid every golden strand. But this woman's hair was wild and free—not braided or covered or restrained in any way. There was something daring and wonderful about such hair, thought Kate. The woman's eyes were serious, yet deep lines in the corners suggested laughter. She wore a coarse brown robe that almost swallowed her slight body. It reminded Kate of Brother Luke's. A heavy rope was knotted round her waist, and on her feet were sandals like the peasants wore. She sat quietly, as though waiting for something.

"I think I know who you are," said Kate at last, throat tight with excitement.

"I think I know who you are, too. Are you surprised?" asked the woman.

Kate stared. "You're Mad Rose, aren't you?"

"I'm Rose, yes. But not mad, I think." The woman smiled, and Kate's face burned with embarrassment.

"I mean . . . I didn't mean . . . I'm sorry."

The woman laughed. "I understand, of course. And I'm so used to 'Mad Rose,' it almost seems my name. But I did want you to be quite clear about the state of my mind."

Kate was enchanted.

"I should ask if I'm right," continued Rose. "You are Kate, aren't you?"

"Yes."

"We have some of the same friends. We'll talk of that later. But now you'd better have something to eat." She unwrapped a linen bundle and offered an oatcake.

"But where . . . I don't understand," stumbled Kate, biting into the cake, which was crisp and delicious. "How did you know I was here?"

"I didn't," answered Rose. "In the mornings I wander the woods. It's a good time to look for plants and berries, and the air is fresh. Not this morning, though," she added. "I don't remember when last it was so sticky. I went to check on a trap I set not far from here," she continued, handing Kate another cake. "On the way back I wanted to drink from the pool, and saw you. I didn't want to frighten you, and was wondering what to do when you saw me."

"Was the trap in a thicket of gorse and blackthorn?"

"Yes. Of course it's poaching, but after all, I must eat. The rope looked as if someone had untied it. Maybe released an animal." She looked at Kate thoughtfully. "It couldn't have been you, by chance?"

Again Kate's face burned, and again she stammered as she tried to explain. "It . . . it was a doe. I fell and looked right into her eyes. Oh, Mistress Rose!" she blurted. "She looked so frightened, and later she ran off with her babies. They came to drink right here at this pool!"

"I'm glad you let her go," said Rose. "I would have done the same. I was hoping to catch a rabbit. But a doe must care for her young this time of year."

"Master Clement told me how brave you are."

"Without him and Brother Luke I might not be alive. And your Grandmother Kate, until she died. It was many years ago . . ." Her voice trailed away, and she seemed lost in thought.

"It was when people thought you were a witch, wasn't it? Why did they think such a terrible thing? I'd never in a thousand years think you a witch!"

Rose laughed. Then she became serious again. "How did you come to be here, child? And why? The parents of Middlethorpe do not permit their maids to wander the woods alone. Are you perhaps looking for some hunters?"

"How do you know that? Have you seen them?"

"Yesterday they passed, not far from here. From what I could tell, they were searching for a dragon. Is it possible?"

"Yes. The dragon of Middlethorpe. He's come back, and they're looking for him."

Rose looked at her thoughtfully for a moment. "Did you know there are two bands of hunters?" she asked.

Kate nodded eagerly. "Did you see them both?"

"I think so. One group was led by someone very tall with dark hair and a beard. There's a friar with them. Could it have been Brother Luke? I caught a flash of his robe through the trees."

"It was! It was Brother Luke! The man with the beard is my father. My brother's with them, too. He's riding a chestnut mare. Oh, Mistress Rose, I'll find them now, I'm sure!"

"The men in the other band were angry and frightened," continued Rose. "They shouted and didn't seem to know what they were doing."

"That's Jankin, the cobbler, and some others who set out on their own," said Kate. "But Father says no one really knows about dragons. I tried to go along," she confided suddenly, "but they caught me, so I had to find another way."

Rose looked at her, astonished, and began to laugh. It was a wonderful laugh, thought Kate. "You tried to go along on the hunt? And in those clothes, I'll wager!" She threw back her head and laughed as though she would never stop. At last she wiped her eyes and pushed the wild hair back from her face. "Tell me," she asked, suddenly serious, "when did all of this begin? And why?"

Kate told her about Fife and the dragon rumors, about the fire in Benningfield, about the unicorn horn and the terrible scene in Master Clement's shop. Rose listened and said nothing.

Kate pulled the ivory casket from her pouch and handed it to Rose. "This is why I'm here. To bring it to the hunters. And also," she added defiantly, "because I want to see the dragon."

Mistress Rose looked at her for a long moment. Then she turned her attention to the little box. "Is this the unicorn horn?" she asked. "The casket is beautifully wrought."

Kate nodded and told her more about her decision to bring it to the hunters.

"Now I know why Master Clement told me of you!" exclaimed Rose. "And how we would be friends if only we could meet! You are brave, my child, and have imagination."

Kate felt a rush of happiness. "I asked Mother to let me meet you. She said it would be dangerous for us both. And Master Clement said the same thing. He also said he loves us both. Why would they wish to keep us apart?"

"It is not always safe to have one's own ideas— and to say them aloud. I think that is the reason." She laughed. "And with two such as we, who knows what damage could be wrought!"

"Mistress Rose!" Kate blurted it out before she could stop herself. "Master Clement told me you think dragons don't exist. Is it true?"

"I confess, I've often wondered."

"But Mistress! Everyone knows there are dragons.

I've heard of them all my life. Why, my Grandfather John died in the same hunt as your . . ." She stopped, full of confusion.

"Don't be ashamed, my dear. I know you are thinking of those tales they tell of me and Hick. That I was responsible for the death of the hunters."

"People say you wanted him killed by the dragon, and that you put a curse on the hunters to make it happen."

"They knew Hick treated me badly. They thought I wished him dead." She stared straight ahead.

"Were they right? Was he cruel to you? Master Clement said so." Kate was amazed at her own daring, but somehow she felt free to say anything to this woman.

"Yes. At times he was cruel to me. Hick blamed me because I bore him no children. He wanted a son. In other ways, too, he was a sad and disappointed man." Rose sat back, clasping her arms around her knees.

"Hick was a man who could think and imagine. But no one wanted a peasant who could think. He turned to drink in his despair. Then he could be violent."

"Why did you stay with him, Mistress?"

"Why stay with him?" she burst out, her eyes blazing. "What choice did I have? I was young, and still behaved as I was expected to." She was silent for a moment, and continued in a calmer voice, "But it is madness to say I put a curse on those hunters. I wouldn't have known how, even if I'd wished it. What people refuse to understand, is that I'm no witch. I am an ordinary woman—different only because I've always spoken my ideas."

"Mistress!" Kate's eyes shone. "I want to be just like you someday."

Rose burst into laughter. "Then, my child, the people of Middlethorpe will have another reason to think ill of me!"

Kate had no answer. "But why don't you think there are dragons?" she asked, returning to their earlier conversation. "How can that be?"

"Child, I've lived in this forest for close to twenty years, and never have I seen a sign of one. I sometimes think we imagine all manner of things in the darkness of our souls. I pray these hunters do not cause more harm than any dragon ever would."

"But how do you explain what happened to those hunters last time? And what of the fire in Benningfield, and the poisoned woman? Or of the dragons that carry away young maids and children? My mother once spent many days in a dark cellar with other young maids so the monster would not carry them off. What of all that?" Kate's mind was in a turmoil. What could Mistress Rose possibly be thinking? And yet . . . there was something about her that Kate could not ignore.

Mistress Rose shook her head thoughtfully. "I'm not sure those hunters were devoured by the dragon, as everyone says." She stopped abruptly. "You'd better forget I said that. Such notions are dangerous. They served to have me driven into the forest."

"Is that why?" Kate was shocked.

"Perhaps not, but they helped."

"But Mistress, what of all the evil that dragons have done? Tim told of a dragon that ate all the maidens in a town—except the daughter of the king," she added.

Mistress Rose answered slowly, choosing her words carefully. "All I can tell you is this. I've seen much evil in my life, but never the evil of dragons. The creatures of the forest live with a sense of order. They know their natural enemies and accept them. And I have lived with them in harmony. The monsters I've known," she burst out, "were clothed in human flesh, not scales and claws. From their mouths have come vicious lies and slander, not fiery breath." She stopped abruptly. "I'm sorry. I've no right to burden you with my anger."

"I've always thought there were dragons, Mistress Rose. And I've always wanted to see one. I even have a parchment at home with a drawing of the real dragon of Middlethorpe. Do you really believe . . ." Kate stumbled, struggling for the right words and the courage to say them. "Are you really saying," her voice dropped to a whisper, "that there is no dragon at all?"

"As I said, I've often wondered. But it's so strange and powerful a notion that people dare not even think on it."

"But what brought you to such an idea, Mistress Rose?"

"You must remember that, living as I do, I spend much time pondering. Sometimes I think that all our talk about the evil of dragons makes it easier to push aside thinking about our own. The evil of men and women. Everyone tells of those terrible and vicious serpents, and dwells on the harm they've done, but I don't know a single person who has ever seen one."

"The abbot says the monk who drew that dragon in the manuscript was drawing our own dragon," said Kate.

"Have you asked the monk himself?" asked Rose.

"He's been dead for many years," said Kate.

"So, once again, no one really knows," said Rose. "But my dear, never ever tell anyone you have such thoughts, or that you talked of them with me. It is dangerous."

"But why?"

Mistress Rose smiled sadly. "Most people are afraid of strange opinions. And the very thought that the dragon—a creature feared far back into the mists of time—may not be real is an idea that strikes terror into most hearts. Always it is easier to deal with fears that we know rather than those we don't. But come!" she said, and this time her smile was not sad. "If you want to reach the hunters before dark, you must be off. I'll walk with you for a time." She sprang to her feet and held out her hand.

"Come with me all the way," pleaded Kate, as she grasped Rose's hand. "If they're hurt you'll know how to care for them . . . and maybe you'll come back with us to Middlethorpe!"

Rose shook her head. "It's too late for that. My home is in the forest now. It broke my heart to leave, but now I couldn't bring myself to return."

"What do you do in the winter, when it's cold? Where do you find shelter—and food?"

Rose had mischief in her eyes. "At times in the winter I've stayed in one of the dragon caves."

"Mistress Rose!" Kate was aghast. "How . . . how could you?"

"The first time I didn't know what it was. Later, when Master Clement told me, I gave it no thought, because nothing had happened to me." She laughed. "But do not worry! I promised Master Clement I would never stay there again. He helped me build a shelter of saplings and rock where I have lived these many years."

"But . . . but what do you eat?" stammered Kate, still almost too shocked to speak.

"I told you about trapping small animals," said Mistress Rose. "And of course berries and roots and fungi. There are all kind of plants in the forest that I cook and eat. I even grow a few. Sometimes I find grain in nearby fields, and in the fall I gather masses of nuts." She stopped to rummage in a large bag tied to the rope round her waist. "You may have no food until you find your hunters, for it's still early in the season for ripe nuts and berries. And you must take great care with mushrooms. Here," she said, "have the rest of these cakes."

Kate thanked her and packed them into her pouch, where the meat pies had been. "Don't you get lonely?" she asked, as they started off once more.

"Not often. At first I did, of course. Sometimes I thought I'd truly go mad. I didn't know how to live in the forest. It was a terrible time."

"What happened?"

"Brother Luke taught me how to dress like this. In the old days, your grandmother came to see me when she could, or sent things I needed with Master Clement when he came on herb-gathering trips. Without them I would have died, I think. Either of illness or loneliness. After all, though people said I was a witch, and that I was mad, I was really like most women."

"Was your hair always . . ."

"Like this? Oh, no! Or they would have run me out far sooner than they did. But after I had lived in the forest for a while, it seemed so free—so natural. Never again could I wear it all tied up, away from the fresh air and the wind!"

As they walked, they heard a low rumbling in the distance. The sun, which had come in and out of the clouds fitfully all day long, vanished. "I believe they were headed for the clearing with the great Druid oak," said Rose. "It's very large. They may be there now. I'll walk with you a bit farther, and then you'll find it by yourself." She gave Kate an encouraging smile. "But before we part, my child, tell me about yourself. During other times, when there's no dragon. What do you like to do? What is your greatest wish?"

Never, thought Kate, had anyone asked about her greatest wish! "I've always wanted to see the dragon," she replied. "Always."

"Do you have friends? One should have friends, you know."

"Daisy is my friend," replied Kate thoughtfully. "But she doesn't always understand. And Geoffrey, of course—that's my brother—but he doesn't either. I think that my best friend is Tim. He has no parents and is apprenticed to the glassblower in the village. He's nice, and he listens, and never makes fun of me. Actually," she said in a rush, "he's wonderful! He plays the flute and sings, and he's helping to make the rose window for Middlethorpe Cathedral." She stopped, out of breath, and Mistress Rose smiled.

"And Master Clement," continued Kate after a moment, suddenly remembering. "Master Clement's going to teach me about herbs." That was my other greatest wish—to learn about herbs and healing. Like my grandmother." She stopped. "And like you!"

"It is my greatest joy," said Mistress Rose. "My greatest wish is to read books. To know more about the lore of healing."

"You, too?" exclaimed Kate. "Always, always I've wanted to read. My brother goes to the abbey school, and he doesn't even like it. But now, Master Clement says I might learn to read in the big books he has in his shop." She looked at Rose. "Perhaps he will teach you, as well."

"It would be a joy above all others," said Rose. "And who knows, perhaps it shall come to pass." She stopped. "But I must leave you now."

"Don't go," pleaded Kate. "There are so many things I want to ask of you. And tell you." She had said nothing about being Master Clement's apprentice! Kate felt the tears sting her eyes. "I'll visit you, Mistress Rose, no matter what. And I'll think on what you said about the dragon."

"You will decide for yourself what you think is the truth. But let our talk about the dragon be our secret." Rose looked at Kate for a long moment. Then she turned abruptly and started back the way they had come. Kate watched until the slight figure had disappeared among the trees, and continued on her way.

The air grew more and more oppressive as Kate pushed along. Her chest felt constricted, but she did not stop to rest. The sun remained hidden, and the distant rumbling grew louder. It sounded like the market carts of Middlethorpe on the cobbles of the square. Kate felt a pang of homesickness that brought back all of the uneasiness she had felt the day before. What was happening in this strange and silent place? Where were the hunters? And the dragon? It was as though the world had stopped breathing. Even worse, the afternoon was drawing to a close, and she might have to spend another night in the forest alone. At the thought, her whole body tightened; her heart pounded with terror.

And then the forest sprang to life. A rushing wind swept through the trees. Large drops of rain cooled Kate's face. Flashes of lightning split the sky. Saplings bent in the wind. Leaves were torn from their branches and whirled to the ground. The sky grew dark. Only the wind could be heard in the strange, unnatural gloom.

Suddenly there was chaos, a roaring in the trees, limbs hurtling to the ground. Light flashed, thunder cracked, rain poured down in splashing sheets of water. Kate threw her arms around the nearest tree, her face pressed against the rough wet bark. She closed her eyes, but a blinding flash penetrated her tightly shut lids. There was a ripping, tearing sound and she saw a great trunk split in half, raw wood bright against the gloom. Kate ran in a panic. She remembered Fife's tales of fire and dragon's breath. Is this what he meant? She stumbled on, when in another burst of light she saw that she had reached the clearing, and there stood the great Druid oak! Kate was safe. But she was alone. There were no hunters to be seen!

Where were they? Could it be that at this moment they were doing battle with the monster? Surely, surely Mistress Rose was wrong! She huddled against the great tree and tried to warm herself with her hood. With a stab of alarm she felt for her pouch. The unicorn casket was safe and dry inside, and Kate

gripped it tightly for comfort and reassurance. If only
the hunters were here! Master Clement had told her
of the Druid oaks, their mysterious strength, their
hallowed shelter. How even the mistletoe and ivy
that hung from their gnarled and twisted branches
held an uncanny power over the forces of evil.

Evil! Another flash leaped through the sky like the
flicking of a serpent's tongue—a dragon's fiery
tongue that scorched and devoured all it touched.
She remembered the peasants' tales of burning
dragon's breath. Perhaps this very storm was the
monster's wrath! A beast roused to fury by the med-
dlesome hunters of Middlethorpe! Was it possible?
Or was it just thunder and lightning and roaring of
the wind? That's what Mistress Rose would say. If
only she were here! She would know whether the
wind was the lashing of the dragon's huge and scaly
tail; the thunder and lightning, howls of rage from
his fiery throat.

Kate called out to the Virgin and all the saints she
could remember. She prayed for the safety of the
hunters, their horses and mules. She prayed for her
father and Geoffrey. She prayed for Rob and Brother
Luke and Janet's Davy. She even prayed for Fife and
the mule, Peterkin. Most of all she prayed for Tim.
Her heart was filled with dread; she was certain the
hunters were in trouble. Then, suddenly, as though
in a dream—but too sharp for a dream—through the
rushing wind and spattering rain she heard the shrilling of a hunter's horn.

10

The Great Druid Oak

The horn! Could it be the hunters? Kate sprang to her feet and ran toward the sound. Where could they be? Suddenly, in the gloom of the rain, she saw something move. A horse broke through a dense thicket at the edge of the clearing. It was the dirtiest, most bedraggled creature Kate had ever seen, its brown-and-white markings almost obliterated by mud, its mane tangled and matted. But it seemed familiar. She looked to see who its rider might be, and her heart stopped. There, drenched and disheveled in the streaming rain, was Tim, his bright hair dark and waterlogged, in his hand a hunter's horn.

"Tim! Oh, Tim!"

He looked around, startled. Then he spied her and his face was radiant. Kate's heart lurched as she ran toward him.

"Kate!" He shook his head as if dazed. "Surely I'm dreaming. Is it really you?" He climbed carefully from the exhausted horse and stood unsteadily. He reached out to clasp her hand, his eyes riveted on her face. "I did dream of you," he said, tugging his sodden hair.

Kate stood, hand in Tim's, expecting to burst with happiness. Tim was safe. And he looked at her with a joy that made her tingle, the green of his eyes startling in his mud-spattered face. "Kate, however did you get here?" Before she could answer, another horse entered the clearing. It was the elegant black mare of Master Simon, now soaked and covered with mud like Tim's brown-and-white mount. Its rider looked even worse than the mare.

"Father!"

"Kate!" Master Simon stared as one possessed, then leaped from his horse. "Kate! My daughter!" He hurried toward her and she rushed to meet his embrace. "What . . . is it . . ." He held her away to look more closely. "This cannot be happening! Are you really here, my daughter, or am I dreaming? And what madness is this? A monster is raging, and we come upon you here alone? Where are the others?"

"There are no others."

"Of course there are others! It is unseemly to joke at such a time! A time when we are all distraught, fresh from battle with the . . ." He broke off. "Where are they? Tell me!"

"Father, I speak truth. I came alone!"

"Alone?" exclaimed her father. "Alone in this dangerous place?" He rubbed his eyes and looked again. "I must be going mad! Surely, surely I dream."

"Father, please don't distress yourself! I am fine, and will tell you everything, but first tell me. Is Geoffrey safe? And where are the others?" Even as Kate spoke, more riders came out of the forest. Some were mounted, some walked beside their limping animals. All were rain-soaked and filthy, with scratches and cuts on their faces and bodies, a far cry from the well-outfitted band that had left Middlethorpe such a short time ago. But it was their manner that struck fear into Kate's heart, for they looked dazed, stunned, as though they had experienced dreadful things.

As they entered the clearing, the rain let up, the thunder and lightning ceased. Suddenly Rob appeared, drenched and dirty like the rest. "By the saints, Miss Kate!" He slid off his mule, wincing with pain, and came to greet her. "I always said you were the pluckiest maid o' them all." He gripped her hand in his two large and calloused ones. "However did you come to find us, Miss, and where are the others?"

Master Simon broke in. "I still cannot believe what I see! Right in the midst of this dragon forest! What possessed your mother to let you go? And Master Clement!"

"Father, please! I'll tell you everything. Mother knew nothing. Nor did Master Clement. But where's Geoffrey?" she asked, searching among the riders who continued to enter the clearing. "And Brother Luke. Are they safe?"

"I pray they're safe! When all have come out of the forest we shall see."

"Father! What happened?"

Master Simon turned away. He seemed unable to speak. Suddenly Kate sensed what she had not been able to explain to herself. It was fear. An aura of fear.

"Did you see the dragon? Is that why you all look so . . ."

"I don't know how to answer you, my daughter. I don't yet know. But one thing I have learned," he continued, his face ashen. "The monster is out there! He's in that forest, not far from where we are standing, and my soul trembles." Kate was stunned. This was her father talking—Master Simon the strong, the practical, the unafraid!

"Was it just now, Father? Tell me! Please! Two days I've searched for you in this forest." She stopped in desperation and whispered, suddenly defeated by his strange manner. "What did you see?"

"Forgive me," said Master Simon at last. "Dreadful, frightening things have happened to us. Things I would never have believed! And just now . . ." He stopped. "But we cannot talk. I must look out for the others. Later you shall know all there is to tell. And I must know what madness brings you here— and alone!" He started for the edge of the clearing, then stopped and hurried back. "Your mother! What of her?" He shook his head, as if dazed. "But it must wait until later."

"Master Clement is with her," said Kate, "and Daisy."

Master Simon nodded. "I must go." He hurried to the edge of the clearing where the hunters continued to straggle out of the forest.

"Kate." Tim spoke in a whisper. "How long have you been here? Was anything amiss? I mean just now, before we came."

"There was a terrible storm, and I found this oak for shelter—not long before I heard your horn."

"Oh, Miss," broke in Rob, "that was the monster! He threw whole trees at us an' burned us with 'is flamin' breath."

"But Rob! All I saw was lightning and rain and breaking trees, and all I heard was noise from the storm!"

"We think it was the dragon," said Tim.

More hunters entered the clearing—several peasants and an apprentice tailor, and Wat, the blacksmith, but still not Geoffrey; still not Brother Luke.

"Where are they, Tim? Where is my brother?"

"Don't worry yourself, Miss. They'll be out in a bit, you'll see," said Rob, but he did not sound convinced.

"Tim. I've brought the unicorn powder." Kate touched the pouch at her waist. "It's in here. I'll give it to Father. It should be used on everyone's wounds."

"Master Clement sent you out here alone?" Tim stared, aghast. "He'd do no such thing!"

"Of course he didn't! He knows nothing, but blamed himself for not giving it to Father. I came without telling anyone. Otherwise they'd never have let me go."

"My Daisy always said you had spirit!" exclaimed Rob. "Not like some other maids in Middlethorpe who put on such fine airs."

"That's true," said Tim, grinning. "But this? I wouldn't've believed it of any maid—nor many a man!"

"If you both think I'm so brave, why won't you tell me what happened in the forest?"

Suddenly Rob lost his composure. "Oh, Miss! We saw the monster. In truth, we did! An' I wonder that you didn't. He was everywhere. The roarin' and the flames! I thought we were in the burnin' furnace of hell! His tail lashed around an' sent huge limbs crashin' down on us. And 'is throat! Oh, Miss, it gaped at me an' I saw rows of teeth as sharp as knives. I ran to get away, and he threw a tree across my path. I tried to get at 'im with my pikestaff, but he passed over me. Then 'e was on top of us again, wings flappin', sendin' down burnin' sticks and branches. We tried to hurt 'im with spears and arrows, but we could not."

Kate listened with growing excitement—and doubt, as she recalled Mistress Rose's words. "Rob. Tim. Are you sure it was the monster? Not all storms are caused by dragons."

"Never, Miss! Never just a storm! It was the work

o' Satan and 'is demons. I c'n say no more. Ask the others. Oh, the shame of it! Thirty strong men go out to kill a dragon. An' look at us—a shamblin', mucky mess! An' lost in the forest, to boot!"

"Sister!" A rain-drenched figure on a ravaged-looking horse had joined them. Geoffrey, at last! "Father said you were here, but I thought he was mad." A ghost of a smile lit his face. "You did it, Kate! I don't know how, but you did it!" Kate saw admiration in his eyes. And respect. They were really friends! She and Geoffrey. Kate nuzzled the chestnut, trying to hide her shock, for she hardly recognized the usually spirited and exquisitely groomed mare. The horse's coat was unkempt, she limped, and her spirit seemed broken.

"Brother! Rob said it was awful."

Geoffrey nodded. "It was the dragon."

"Are you sure?"

"I'm sure."

"I was in a storm, too. A terrible one."

"Kate, you should've been there. We were picking our way through the forest earlier today when the storm broke. That's all we thought it was at first, just a simple storm. The air was so close I thought I'd choke, and then suddenly there was a roaring wind. And rain. And thunder and lightning. Suddenly there was the monster! We were surrounded by fire and horrors of all kinds. We brandished our weapons to keep him at bay. Here's Brother Luke. He'll tell you."

The friar had already dismounted and was walking toward them. "My daughter! You are a brave and foolish maid, indeed!"

Kate ran to meet him. "Brother Luke, do you think it was the dragon?"

"There was evil in the air. One could sense it, smell it, touch it. Never have I felt so close to Satan. I pray I never shall again." The friar crossed himself.

Without warning the rain began again. It swept down in sheets. Lightning flashed. A roar of thunder rocked the ground.

"Quick!" Tim grasped Kate's hand. "Under the oak! It's the only safe place!" They ran through the newly lashing storm toward the great tree. A flash of lightning almost blinded them. And then a crack and a roar so overpowering that it knocked Kate to the ground. There was a wrenching tearing sound as though the whole forest was being ripped apart. The earth shook and trembled, and a great roar of wind swept over the clearing. Kate, shielding herself from flying debris, rolled over on her stomach and sheltered her head in her arms. She could feel Tim's protective arm around her. Again the earth shook. Then silence. She opened her eyes and looked across the clearing. She closed her eyes and looked again. But she had not been mistaken. The great Druid oak—island of shelter and safety—was split from top to bottom.

11

Terror at the Bog

One half of the great tree had crashed to the ground, filling the clearing with its vast, leafy bulk. For a moment there was a stunned silence. Then everyone sprang to life.

"It's the dragon! He's still after us!"

"But this is the sacred oak!"

"Only our Lord in heaven has power over the dragon," said Brother Luke.

"Away from this place!"

"Not even the great oak is safe from the monster!"

"The dragon has overpowered its magic! Hurry!"

Tim rushed off with a guildsman to keep several panicking hunters from scattering into the woods. Kate and Geoffrey helped Rob with the animals. Horses and mules brayed and screamed, their terrified eyes staring wildly in the gloom. Dogs barked and raced around, their spiked collars a danger to all in their path.

"Men, stay together!" shouted Master Simon. "Do not run off alone!"

Harry pulled him aside. "Let's do battle with the monster here, Master. We know he lurks in the forest just beyond the clearing. Why run now when we almost have him?"

"No, Harry. The men are in a panic. They need rest, and time to regain control. Our chance of victory will be better if we wait."

The innkeeper exploded in anger. "You are soft, Master! Soft and without judgment! I'll do as you order, but i' faith, I pray we don't live to regret this day!" He turned abruptly and strode off.

Master Simon watched him for a moment, shaking his head. Kate, who had heard the exchange, hurried to his side. "Father! Why is the innkeeper so filled with hate?"

"Don't let him trouble you, my daughter. We've all been through terror these days, and it takes its toll."

Kate persisted. "But it was Harry who pleaded with you to lead the hunt!"

"Electing a leader is easy, my dear. The hard thing is to follow that leader's judgment when you don't agree with him." Master Simon smiled down at her and took her arm. "It is certainly foolish of me, and perhaps selfish, but I'm glad you are with us. Come now, let us leave this place." Never, thought Kate with a glow, had she felt so close to her father!

The men hurried their animals across the clearing, entering the forest on the opposite side from where they had left it such a short time before, climbing over branches and debris, away from the shattered oak. Kate and Geoffrey followed with Tim's horse and the chestnut, and found Tim waiting for them. The hunters struck more deeply into the woods, faster and faster, only away from the terrible monster who would give them no peace. Kate remembered the woods she had entered only the day before, so dappled with light and shadow, so friendly, so peaceful, so fragrant with the rich smell of earth and growing things. This was different. It was more like the forest she had been warned against all of her life: murky and dim, menacing and evil, an atmosphere that struck her with a chill of terror.

Gradually, a horrible reek of corruption and rot filled the air. With a stab, Kate remembered her mother's tale of sickening odors and shadows flying overhead. Was this, then, the dragon, after all? This smell of evil—this was something new! She looked up, but trees blotted out the sky. Could it be the dragon—the dragon of Middlethorpe—high above those treetops, ready to swoop down and destroy them? Suddenly she wanted to tell Geoffrey—tell Tim—about Mad Rose's words. She needed to tell someone! "Brother," she said, "Tim, listen," when a shriek rent the air, a shriek so wild that they froze. Another. And then a scream—the terrified braying of a mule—that sent shivers of horror up Kate's back.

"By the saints, what was that?" Geoffrey clutched her arm.

"Sh-sh-sh. Listen."

A voice shouted, "If anyone's out there, come no

closer! For God's sake, come help us, but take care! There's a bog!"

"Where?" shouted Master Simon. "Where is this bog?" He was cut off by another shriek so bloodcurdling that the chestnut reared in terror.

"What's that? Who are you?" shouted Master Simon.

"Jankin, the cobbler, from Middlethorpe! In the name of God, hurry, whoever you are!"

"I'm Simon, the wool merchant, with a band of hunters. Who's in the bog?"

"Fife and his mule!" shouted the cobbler. "Be careful of soft ground. And be quick! Don't bring your animals. They'll sink!"

A voice close beside her made Kate jump. "He's just ahead, Master. I've come to guide ye." It was the fishmonger. "Oh, Master, it's awful! The peddler's almost up to 'is shoulders, and there's nothin' we c'n do! The ground's muck, and there's no bottom to it."

"Stay with the animals!" called Master Simon to some of the men. "You heard Jankin. Come no closer!"

Another shriek curdled the air. "It's the mule," said the fishmonger. "He broke through first. An' Fife got caught when 'e tried to save 'im." A sudden fury overcame him. "It's the dragon done it! It'd never have happened if that monster hadn't come at us with 'is fire and flame. That mule'd never've gone off steppin' out like that. Take care!" he yelled, breaking out of the trees into a large clearing. "Take care where ye step! I was talkin' an' didn't watch. Here's the bog."

Kate looked out over a large area clear of trees or shrubs. The dim, open space seemed to heave and bubble, and from it rose a sickening odor of decay. Suddenly, not far from where she stood, Kate saw the struggling man and the frantic beast. But it might as well have been the other side of the bog, for all they could do to help, for already the ground was treacherous, and Kate could feel it give slightly beneath her feet. Any step farther out might mean the same plight for them as that of poor, desperate Fife and the wild-eyed Peterkin.

Jankin was stretched flat on the soft, fetid ground, much farther out than he should have dared. The ground heaved slightly beneath his weight, but a low tangle of groundcover kept him from sinking. He held out a lance to the peddler, who struggled to catch hold. Although, thought Kate in despair, even if Fife were to get a grip, he would never be able to pull himself out of the sucking, clinging slime, which was already up to his armpits.

"Save Peterkin!" screamed the peddler. "Don't mind me! Help the poor beast. He got no arms to keep himself above the muck!"

"Grab the lance, man!" shouted Jankin. "Don't give up!"

"I can't!" The peddler stretched out his arms, but even as Kate watched, he seemed to sink deeper.

"Let me!" Kate lay flat on the spongy ground, and inched her way to the cobbler. "I'm lighter."

"Kate! No!" Tim grabbed her from behind, and pulled her back.

"Go back!" shouted Jankin. "Don't be a fool!"

"Leave me!" Kate shook off Tim. She grabbed a spear and crawled several spans farther than Jankin out on the trembling surface of the bog.

"Fife! Grab this!"

"I can't!" The peddler was weeping. "Please, please save my Peterkin!"

Peterkin screamed, head swinging from side to side above the muck.

"The mule!" shouted Fife. "Don't let 'im drown!"

Peterkin's scream was broken off by a terrible gurgling sound. "He's swallowin' the slime! Oh, my Peterkin! My soul! Why'd I bring you to this cursed place?" The peddler lashed about, and the men near the edge of the bog lay flat, pushed out lances and poles for the mule to grip between his teeth; for the peddler to grasp.

In a last desperate effort, some of them slid out, close to sinking themselves, when suddenly, without warning, a blast of wind hurled down upon them. Those who stood were knocked off their feet. Once more rain streamed, thunder cracked, lightning pierced the ground and flashed into the bog. Something hit Kate on the shoulder, but she scarcely noticed. Lightning blinded her. A curdling scream pierced the air, and then a sucking—a gurgling. Then nothing. Silence. When Kate opened her eyes, all were staring in horror at the empty surface of the bog.

"They're gone." It was Tim, now beside her on the stinking, mucky ground.

"The bog swallowed them. Oh my God." One of the guildsmen spoke for the horrified hunters nearby.

"What've I done?" Tears made tracks down Jankin's slime-covered face. "It was me! I lured him to this awful place."

Kate looked again. There was no trace of Fife or the mule.

"He's gone." Jankin spoke tonelessly. "They're both gone. There's naught to be done. Nothing."

"It was the dragon!" screamed Davy. "The fishmonger's right. The dragon done it! He knew we were helpless, an' killed 'em to teach us a lesson. Let's get away from this place!"

"We'll return to the clearing and think what to do," said Master Simon. "Away from this bog before another of us gets caught! Even the clearing is safer than this."

"We were fools to leave it in the first place!" Harry, the innkeeper, looked hard at Master Simon. "By now we might be done with battle, and the monster dead before us."

"Follow yonder stream," said Jankin. "It'll take you back. I'll stay the night with the peddler. His blood is on my head. It's the least I can do."

"Don't," pleaded Geoffrey. "Come with us. Away from this dragon-cursed place."

"Let him be," said Brother Luke, gently pulling Geoffrey away. "It is something he must do to be at peace with himself. Come," he said to the others. "Let us return."

"I'll follow when dawn breaks," said Jankin, and sat down to start his vigil.

12

Night of the Dragon

Stumbling over roots, they pushed their way through the soaking underbrush, the mucky ground, the rain-drenched trees. Geoffrey was with Master Simon, trying to calm Harry, the innkeeper, who still argued for a different course of action. Kate followed Tim, who was murmuring words of encouragement to his exhausted horse. How gentle he was, thought Kate. With people and with animals alike. And how happy she always was to be with him—even here, in the terrible dragon forest.

The hunters, weary and wet, and too long without rest, were in a state of shock. Some raged and cursed, some wept, some stared blankly ahead, not uttering a word. It was almost dark. The eerie stillness was broken only by the hunters and the water dripping from a thousand trees. The forest became less dense, and there was room for Kate and Tim to walk side by side.

"It's like a cathedral," said Tim softly, looking up

at the vast canopy of trees. "The quiet, and the gloom—"

"And the wet," said Kate, shaking the drops from her hair.

Tim grinned. "Well, yes. That too. But look at the colors. All the greens and grays. The shadows and shapes. Oh," he exclaimed, "I love this forest. And all my life I've heard naught save how fearsome and terrible it is!"

Kate looked at him, stifling a shiver of fear. "Remember, it still may be. We may yet run into that monster. And what about this morning—when you did battle?"

"This morning," he said in wonder. "It already seems days ago. But you are right. Surely I ought to feel terror at this moment. After last night and this morning, after the bog, after Fife and Peterkin. But all I can think of is this forest—beautiful, calm, at peace."

"You remind me of Mistress Rose!" blurted out Kate.

"Mistress Rose? Who's that?"

"She lives in the forest, and never wants to leave." Kate told Tim the whole story, and he was entranced. But she said nothing about the dragon, and what Mistress Rose had said about the monster. Then the woods became nearly impenetrable once more, and Tim dropped back to walk in single file.

It seemed to Kate the journey would never end. She was tired, and stumbled over roots and underbrush. Unlike Tim, who found them filled with beauty and peace, she found the silent woods uncanny after the horrors of the day. Every crackling branch, every unexpected sound caused her to jump. She looked for strange shadows, for watchful eyes in the mist. Where was the monster? If there was a monster, she reminded herself. Was he, perhaps, watching them this very moment, waiting to pounce?

They continued single file, some of the hunters mounted, others on foot leading their horses or mules. As they worked their way through the darkening forest, Kate heard once again the screaming Peterkin, the pleading, weeping Fife. Again she saw the sinister expanse of the silent, trembling bog, hiding its secrets beneath the stinking crust. It was a strench that seemed to permeate everything even now, bringing back all she had ever heard about the disgusting smells that heralded dragons. She felt like the hunters, who were ready to fall in their tracks from exhaustion and despair. If only they would reach the clearing! If only they could rest! If only the monster had finally done his worst!

And what if Mistress Rose was right? What if the dragon was of their own imaginings? What if all of this, the bog, Peterkin, Fife, all the horrors of this terrible day had naught—nothing at all—to do with the fearsome dragon of Middlethorpe? Kate shook her head to clear it. Never in her life had she felt so helpless—so confused.

And then, for a third time, the forest went wild! A flash brighter than the sun threw them headlong to the ground. Tim was sprawled beside her. "Kate, you were right! The monster's been following us!"

The hunters were in a panic.

"He's back!"

"We're trapped!"

"He's been after us all day!"

"This time he'll get us, for certain!"

"Nay!" yelled the innkeeper. "It's us that'll get him! Is everyone here soft as a pudding?" He sprang to his feet.

"Come men, do battle!" Master Simon shouted above the cracking thunder, his voice almost lost in the uproar. Kate watched as he climbed a tree stump, high, so the men could hear. Let the innkeeper listen now! she thought, silently applauding her father. "Get up," shouted Master Simon. "Fight, every man of you! We are dragon hunters from Middlethorpe, and we'll not go back empty-handed!" He leaped from the stump and grabbed his lance.

"Come at me, serpent!" shouted Geoffrey. "Come at me, and you'll feel my spear!"

"Wait!" shouted Tim, grabbing his flail. He looked anxiously at Kate. "Please, take care!" And was gone, running to catch up with Geoffrey before she could think what to say. The weary hunters groaned and cursed, but they pulled themselves up and clutched their weapons. Even as Kate watched, they seemed to gather new courage and strength. She huddled against a thick-trunked beech, fingers digging into the sodden bark. The sky was blocked out by crowns of ancient trees and mist, split only by the day-bright flash of lightning; the roll and crack of thunder; the ripping and tearing of trees and, all at once, the clash of weapons! On every side pikestaffs lashed out, lances were brandished, arrows flew. Kate saw Tim swing his flail wildly in all directions. He's no fighter, she thought, watching him struggle. Nor is he a coward, she added with pride.

Geoffrey hoisted his spear and threw. It flew in a glittering arc—and fell to the ground. He ran to retrieve it. "Here, monster! Into your teeth!" The spear flew again, this time high into a tree—and dangled in the rain-wet branches.

"Up there!" shouted Kate. Cursing, Geoffrey clambered after it, yanked it out in a fury. "Serpent! You'll not escape me again! Here!" He threw wildly. The spear flew—and landed short.

"Let me!" Tim rushed to help Geoffrey, but was pushed aside by the innkeeper, who came with his longbow. Suddenly Kate heard a strangely familiar sound. An eerie crackling that sent chills down her spine. Fire! She watched in horror as flames leaped from tree to rain-drenched tree, small at first and timid, then larger and bolder.

"There he is!" shouted Harry. "I'll get the monster! Watch me!" He raised his bow as the flames licked and darted around him. "Take this!" An arrow zinged past Kate's ear. "And this! And this!" shouted the innkeeper in a frenzy.

"Harry!" screamed Kate. "Stop!" She leaped aside, barely missing another arrow. "Brother Luke! You'll get hit!"

Arrows whizzed and spears flew through the wild, now flaming forest. Flails and pitchforks lashed out and stabbed the air in all directions. Kate's nostrils and throat stung from the heat and soot. The clash of weapons and the curses of the battling hunters made an unholy din. Burning branches flew through the smoke-filled air. Kate slapped at her hair and clothing to smother the sparks. Why, why had she come? What good had she thought she could do in this terrible place? Why had she ever thought she wanted to see the dragon of Middlethorpe!

"Serpent! Into your hide!" One of the guildsmen, his livery in tatters, took aim and shot.

"I've been hit! The monster's attacked me!" Davy screamed, holding his arm. "Help me, someone!"

"Davy! I'm coming!" Kate tried to reach him, but was wracked by a spasm of coughing and could not move. When it had passed, she saw through clouds of billowing smoke that Tim had come to his aid.

"Oh, Miss!" Rob was beside her, his face smeared with blood and soot. "D'you see 'im now? His flappin' wings, his lashin' tail?" Rob brandished his staff, eyes shut against the glare and scorching heat.

"Rob! You'll hit someone!" Kate rubbed her stinging eyes. Another fit of coughing wracked her body. "I don't know!" she croaked, scarcely able to speak. "The smoke burns my eyes and blots out everything!"

"Right there, Miss! Watch! I'll hit him! Into your side, serpent!" He stabbed into the flames, and fell, still clutching his staff. "By the saints, you won't escape me this time!" He sprang to his feet and lashed out again.

The clamor was dreadful. Kate's eyes felt on fire, her lips were cracked, and she could barely swallow. In a trance, she looked out at the wild unreality of the scene. It was like nothing she could have imagined. Nothing like the little dragon on the parchment. Much, much worse. Much more terrible! Perhaps Rose was all wrong. Perhaps she had never seen the monster like this. For what could this be but the monster? That sinuous shadow his wing. That blinding flash his treacherous, flaming jaw. Those darting red and orange points—the dragon's teeth.

"Sister! Watch! This time I'll get him!" Geoffrey rushed off, spear ready to thrust.

Kate's head roared. In a stupor she watched as the flames coursed ever more wildly through the rain-drenched trees, creating a furnace of darting fire. The men plunged through the crackling heat and light, shrieking, yelling, cursing the monster who escaped their every thrust. She looked for Tim, but could not see him or Davy through the billows of smoke. As though in a dream she heard her father, encouraging the hunters, calling out commands and instructions, but he, too, was not visible through the chaos that surrounded her.

And then, suddenly, she saw the dragon! She knew it! Through the smoke-clouded air, through an inferno of flying sparks and burning branches, she saw him! Deep within the leaping flames she saw his teeth, his flashing, lashing tail, the dark notched spine of his scaly back, his red and orange, gold and shiny back, his tail and flaming jaw, and the razor-sharp teeth, row on row.

She clutched her throbbing head. "Tim!" she screamed. "The dragon! He's over there!" She grabbed someone by the arm. "Look!" Her head whirled and the forest spun around her. It was Master Simon who pulled her away from the flames, and shouted, "Men! Follow me! Or we perish!"

The flames licked their way through the underbrush, following them, coming closer. Harry, the innkeeper, raised his longbow in the eerie light. "You fools, don't run! We've got him! We can't leave now!"

"I've had enough!" exclaimed a guildsman, throwing down his weapon. "I'm with you, Master!"

"Don't go!" shouted Geoffrey. "Harry's right. We've got him where we want him." He ran to the innkeeper's side, spear raised high.

"Do you want us all to be destroyed—like last time? Think of your own grandfather, for the love of the saints!" Master Simon shouted above the roar of the fire. "Come, we'll look for the monster again. If we stay now, he'll devour us!"

"We've got him now, and I'm staying. Go. Go with

the master. You're all cowards!" Harry flung it at them. Geoffrey, a few steps away, aimed his spear when a huge, fiery tree flew through the burning air, cutting off Harry's speech, crashing to earth in flames where the innkeeper had stood but a moment before.

"Harry's in there. The monster threw that tree on 'im!"

"I c'n see the dragon!" screamed Davy. "Look at 'is head. I c'n see his teeth! Right there in the flames. He's devourin' Harry!"

"He defied that dragon, and that dragon killed 'im! Let's get away from 'ere!"

"Geoffrey!" Kate, in a daze, stumbled toward her brother. "Come away! He'll devour you, too!" She struggled to pull him back, but he wrenched himself free. "Brother! You'll die!"

"Don't any of you care about Harry?" screamed Geoffrey, weeping with rage and frustration. "Help him!" He prodded at the burning tree with his spear, trying desperately to move the huge trunk, trying to find the innkeeper in the inferno. "Don't pull me away, for God's sake! Come help!"

"I'm with ye, lad!" shouted the fishmonger. "Ye're all a bunch of cowards, and ye need a boy to show ye the way!" He stabbed at the burning tree with his pitchfork. "Here, lad, I'll help ye! Harry," he yelled, "we'll kill the monster an' save ye!"

"Watch out!" yelled someone, as a huge branch flew through the air.

"Fishmonger! Move!"

"Brother! Down!" Kate's warning was an instant too late. Geoffrey's body, struck by a flying branch, crumpled to the ground. She grabbed his fallen spear and tried to pry the heavy branch from his body. One end flared up, showering debris into her face. She doubled over and lost her grip on the weapon. Scrambling for it, she looked up—into the fiery jaws of the dragon! She saw deep into his burning throat, orange and red, with teeth like pointed flames, leaping and flashing—ready to devour her brother!

The creature's fiery tail lashed out. She could see his spiny back, his jointed wings. The dragon of her parchment! As she struck at some sparks on her tunic, her hand touched the purse at her waist. The casket! The unicorn horn! How could she have forgotten! Now! Now was the time to use it. In a frenzy she ripped open her purse and groped for the little box. Please, Master Clement, she breathed, please let it be as you said. Please! And let it save Geoffrey. She pulled out the casket and fumbled with the catch; tried to grasp a handful of the precious powder—the magic unicorn horn. The lid stuck; she struggled desperately to open it. Finally, with a wild swing of her arm she hurled the whole thing at the dragon. It hit a tree and flew open, scattering the magic powder into the monster's raging throat!

There was a moment of total silence. It was as though the world had stopped. Then a roar of flame. Kate tried to reach her brother, but was flung back, staggering, into the underbrush. Half-stunned, she clutched a sapling and watched as floods of rain poured onto the flames—like gigantic buckets of water into an open fire. Huge clouds of smoke and steam enveloped the scene, with noise like the hissing of a thousand demons, and a shooting of sparks into the fire-blackened trees. The rain came down in streams, in sheets, in gushes. The dragon spurted new columns of flame, new bursts of fire, sent new showers of debris through the air. But the water continued to pour from the heavens—until every trace of the fiery monster was gone. And then, as suddenly as it had begun, the downpour ceased. The roaring noise died away. The hissing subsided. Silence descended on the ravaged forest. The dragon of Middlethorpe was gone.

"Geoffrey!" Instantly Kate was at his side.

He opened his eyes and looked at her in confusion. "What happened?"

She watched as he tested his arms and legs, moving them gingerly, trying to sit up. "Oh Brother, I thought you were dead!" She dabbed at a cut on his face.

"I can scarcely believe it," said Geoffrey. "Nothing seems broken. Nor am I burned. It's the unicorn horn," he said in amazement. "I'd not be alive without it!"

"Kate!" Tim rushed to her side. "What happened? What did you do?"

"She threw the unicorn horn. At the dragon!

Didn't you, Miss?" Rob and the others gathered around.

"Into the jaws of the monster!" exclaimed Brother Luke. "You've driven him away. And saved your brother's life!"

"The dragon's gone! Just look around you and see!" Master Simon stood, awed. "Driven away by the magic powder!"

"Is that what happened?" Geoffrey looked at Kate and Tim, who were kneeling beside him. "Was it the unicorn horn, Sister?"

Suddenly Kate felt uncomfortable, embarrassed. "I had to do something, and it was all I had. Master Clement told me of its power."

"We c'n go home!" screamed Davy. "The monster's dead! Oh, Miss, you're a marvel! A marvel's what you are!"

"We must take care," warned Brother Luke. "For a moment the dragon has retreated." He turned to Master Simon. "But let us be cautious and wait a little longer. He's come back three times today to haunt us. And none of us knows the power of the horn."

Rob whispered to Kate, "You saved us, Miss. Saved us from that beast! Wait 'n' see if I'm not right! He's gone, an' you did it with that unicorn powder!"

Kate looked at the smoking, stinking, sodden desolation around them. What had happened to her? What had she seen? Her head was clear from the drenching downpour. The dizziness and roaring were gone. She looked where the monster had writhed and raged, a mass of leaping flame. All she saw now were blackened heaps of branches, charred saplings, stumps of trees at the spot where Geoffrey had lain, struck down by the dragon—but had it been the dragon or a branch? At the spot where, moments before, she had flung the magic powder into the jaws of the serpent—but had it been the serpent, or just the roaring fire?

"What of Harry?" asked Tim.

For a moment Kate did not understand, but Geoffrey nodded, and Brother Luke, who was near, heard. They gathered the men around the ruined trees that were the charred and blackened tomb of the brave innkeeper, and Brother Luke spoke a prayer. "Later we must give him a proper burial. But for now . . ." Master Simon broke in. "For now we leave him as he is. We must leave this place in all haste."

"This dragon-haunted place," muttered the friar. "May the Lord have mercy on his soul!"

They ran from the grave of the innkeeper. They ran from the madness of the dragon forest, no longer swirling with soot and ash and fiery branches, but vile with the smell of smoke and death. They hurried through the woods as fast as they could manage with the wounded men and animals, fleeing the monster who was vanquished for the moment, but still at large for all they knew.

They guided themselves by the little stream, pushing their way along its banks until they reached the clearing of the great Druid oak—no longer a place of shelter and safety, but of ruin, destroyed by the fearful monster's wrath. Still, for the moment they could rest. Exhausted beyond caring, the hunters scattered on the grass. They slept.

Kate lay down beside the ruined oak. She and Tim had made a bed of moss for Geoffrey, helped him lie down, and waited with him till he slept. Suddenly she felt every muscle and tendon of her own aching body, but though she was tired, her head was clear. She looked at Tim, already asleep, and thought back over the battle. She saw herself as she had been— dazed from the scorching heat of fire, head spinning from the noise and clash of weapons, beyond terror in the violence of the storm. At one point she had been sure she was looking at the hideous monster; had been certain he was there in the flame and roar of the night. But had he been? Had he been, really? Why had it looked like naught save burned branches and trees where the dragon had been, once the leaping flame was gone? And what of the unicorn powder? Had its magic really brought about the drenching rain? If only Mistress Rose were here! She would know.

Kate looked at the sleeping hunters, the tranquilly grazing horses and mules, the dogs stretched out, their muzzles between torn and bleeding paws. She looked again at Tim, red hair streaked with mud and ashes, face relaxed in sleep, and wanted to wake him. Wake him and tell him about Mad Rose's words. But she could not bring herself to do it, he looked so peacefully asleep after the endless, terrifying day. Besides, Mistress Rose had asked her to keep silence. Another time, thought Kate, yawning uncontrollably.

Her eyes would not stay open. She tried to push thoughts of the monster from her mind, and remembered Tim's ballad about the unicorn. And what Master Clement had told her of the mysterious and beautiful creature, the messenger of goodness and love. Would she ever see him? Kate wondered. Was he in the forest, too, or had the dragon's evil kept him at bay? She wrapped the liripipe of her hood around her neck for warmth, tried to find a comfortable spot for her bruised and aching body, and slept.

13

A Vision at Dawn

Kate looked out into a mist-enshrouded world. Gauzy billows of white coiled around dark shapes of trees and shrubs. The forest was dim in the early morning light. No sound disturbed the silence, not even the call of a bird. Shivering in the damp, she watched the tendrils and wisps that drifted through the clearing, forming and re-forming into ghostly shapes and patterns. One mass of white looked more substantial than the hazy eddies around it, assuming the shape of a beast. Kate sat quietly, not moving a muscle, hardly daring to breathe. The creature was the shape and size of a horse, and his bearing was regal. The head was long and delicate, his coat a dazzling white. He had a small beard, and his cloven hooves looked polished in the morning mist. Most wonderful was his horn—a single shaft of creamy alabaster that grew from his forehead and spiraled to a point. He stood, an austere and silent presence, glowing faintly through the mists of the dawn-lit clearing. Kate knew she was looking at a unicorn.

He came no closer, but stood alert, head high, ears flicking at the slightest nuance. He had come to protect the hunters. Kate knew it in a flash! He stood silent, unmoving, watching over the sleeping men scattered around on the grass. Suddenly his head turned slightly, as though beckoning to Kate. She rose, and together they left the clearing and headed toward the brook that had guided the hunters the night before. The water was still high from the storm, but no longer overflowed its banks.

Each side of the little stream was lined with the animals of the forest. On the far bank, Kate spied her own little doe with the two fawns. Beside them stood a handsome buck, and not far away, an immense old boar, dark and bristly, with splintered yellow tusks. Rabbits sniffed the air with mobile noses, and squirrels skittered about. A fox sat nearby with his mate and three playful kits.

Up in the trees, Kate saw flocks of birds and several sleep-ruffled owls. Down below, a family of woodcocks peeped out of the brush. There were no wolves, but Kate thought she saw yellow eyes glittering in the mist.

When the animals spied the unicorn, all was silent. Not a whisker stirred; not a feather was ruffled. The only sound was the rushing of the little brook. The forest creatures waited. The unicorn stood at the bank, head high, horn piercing the mist, a royal creature surrounded by his subjects. What had Master Clement said? The forest animals looked on the unicorn as one set apart—a beast with special powers. He cleansed and purified their drinking water, protecting them from the foulness and poison of serpents and dragons.

Even as Kate recalled the words of the apothecary, the unicorn dipped his horn into the stream. He swirled it in a circle, lifted it out dripping, and stood motionless, regarding the creatures, who were watching in awed silence. Then he repeated the ceremony two more times. He remained for a moment, a royal being, accepting the silent tribute of the animals. Presently he turned to Kate, ready to return to the clearing. Already the woodland creatures were drinking from the newly cleansed stream.

Back in the clearing, the unicorn stood as before, guardian of the sleeping band of hunters. Kate sat near the shattered oak, resting her head against a fallen branch, watching him, mysterious and beautiful, shimmering white against the rain-dark forest.

Suddenly there was a call. "Hallo! Hallo!" She opened her eyes and looked into the morning freshness of a rain-washed, sun-bright day. A figure stumbled into the clearing. It was Jankin. The unicorn was gone.

14

The Bog Reveals Its Secret

Kate looked carefully, but it was so. A moment before, the unicorn had stood proud and solitary, keeping watch over the tattered band of hunters and their weary animals. And in a flash—the blink of an eye—he had vanished. The sun was up, shedding its light across the clearing. Where was the mist-drenched morning? And where was the unicorn? Could she have dreamed it? Kate rubbed her eyes, but when she opened them, the dragon-haunted night might never have been, except for the battle-torn hunters and the great shattered oak—and Jankin, shambling and weary, making his way across the clearing.

Kate felt a terrible sadness—as though she had lost something rare and precious. Something that had slipped through her fingers and vanished without a trace. She wished she could tell someone of the magical unicorn, and knew it would be Tim. She looked at him, just beginning to stir. He might not understand, but he would never laugh.

She whispered his name softly, for she did not want to wake the others. Jankin had seated himself, back against a fallen log, until the hunters should wake. Fortunately he had not seen her, hidden as she was by one of the great oak's leafy limbs, higher than she herself, though it lay on the ground, split and broken.

Tim stirred and opened his eyes.

"Wake up. There is something I must ask you."

"What is it?" He shook his head, trying to pull himself out of a bottomless well of sleep. "Kate, is something amiss?"

She came closer and spoke in a whisper. "Did you see something early this morning? Not long ago?"

He looked at her, puzzled. "See something? What do you mean? I was asleep until this very moment."

"Something rare and beautiful," said Kate. "Right here in the clearing. I must know," she said urgently.

Tim shook his head. "I saw nothing," he answered. "I slept through the night until you woke me just now. Of what do you speak?"

Kate hesitated. "I . . . don't think me mad," she implored. She looked at him, undecided whether to continue.

"What? Tell me!" Tim was now fully awake. "What did you see?"

She gathered her courage and blurted it out. "I believe I saw the unicorn! The magical unicorn. Just before the sun rose, in clouds of mist. Right here in this clearing."

Tim stared. "The mysterious unicorn of which we spoke the night of your father's return?"

She nodded, eyes wide. "Right there." She pointed. "The clearing was filled with a white, swirling mist. And suddenly, even as I watched, there he stood. Oh, Tim," she breathed. "He glowed, and stood proud and straight, keeping watch over us all."

"And then?" Tim asked her, transfixed by the tale. He was not scoffing! It gave her the courage to tell everything, just as it happened.

"But didn't you see him?" she asked. "Or us," she continued in confusion, "when we came back from the little brook?"

"I saw nothing, and remember nothing. Did you think I was awake? Is that why you ask?"

Kate thought back. "Everyone was sleeping," she said. "But I do not remember that I looked at you directly. Things were in a mist . . . a blur . . . all save what I told you. Tim, was I awake? I thought I was," she said, trying to visualize each tiny moment. "Or could I have been dreaming?" She shook her head, as though to shake the mist from her brain. "But I must have been awake!"

"You know the old tales," said Tim. "The unicorn appears to rare maids in the forest. Here we are, in the very depths of the forest, and you," he continued, "are an exceedingly rare maid." He looked flushed and awkward. "Why, then, should it not have happened as you said?" he added, rumpling his hair furiously.

Kate's heart leaped. She had been right about Tim. But more than she would have dared to imagine!

By now Jankin had noticed that someone was stirring, and was crossing the clearing toward them.

"Thank you," was all she had time to whisper. "Say nothing of this."

Jankin nodded a greeting and slumped on the ground, placing a short wooden rod on the ground next to him. Kate wondered idly what it might be, but was in no mood to ask. Her feelings toward Jankin were gentler since the events of the bog, but she still distrusted him and feared his bitter tongue. And she could not forget his vicious attack on Master Clement.

"By the saints!" exclaimed the cobbler. "What's been happening?" He looked around the clearing at the sleeping hunters. "You, too! You're all of you blackened with ashes and soot, and soaking wet, to boot! On my way here, I walked through places that looked like hell itself! Was it the dragon, then? Did he follow you back here?"

Kate and Tim told him everything that had happened. It was strange, but the vision of the unicorn had almost driven it from her mind! She had to struggle to recall the dreadful events of the previous day. "And then Kate threw Master Clement's unicorn horn," said Tim, finishing the story, "and the monster was gone!"

Jankin sighed. "And if I'd had my way before I came out here, you'd have had none of that powder last night, and might all have perished." He spoke abruptly, with difficulty, looking at Kate out of the corner of his eye. "Thanks for your care of the master that night. I saw you take him away."

Kate said nothing. Tim listened and made no comment.

Jankin shook his head sadly. "Why should you have aught to say to me? You've no reason to trust me. I made fun of you, and insulted your father. And you saw me that night in Master Clement's shop." He spoke so quietly that Kate could scarcely hear him. "But, in truth, I never meant to do him harm."

"You were terrible to the master," said Kate, his brutal behavior still fresh in her mind. "But his wound was an accident."

"Accident? Anger's more like it—anger, and too much ale." He rubbed his eyes, red-rimmed from lack of sleep. "That's why I had to stay with Fife last night. Without me he'd still be alive. And when I think I almost killed the apothecary . . ." He grimaced at the memory and shook his head.

"You didn't know there was a bog. No one did." Why was she trying to comfort the hated cobbler?

"But I dragged those men into the forest. Sometimes I think there's a curse on me!"

"Fife didn't need to go with you. It was his choice." A few days ago she would have responded with scorn. But this was a different Jankin.

"He couldn't say no. His will wasn't strong

enough. I took advantage of his weakness." Jankin sighed deeply. "And his greed."

"What did you tell him?" asked Tim.

"That if we found the dragon before the others, we'd get his treasure. Gold and jewels and precious stones. Maybe even the pearl in his forehead, if we put him to death. Fife loaded that mule with so many sacks, the poor beast could hardly walk. That's why he sank so quickly."

"Sacks?"

"To carry back the treasure."

"That's why you went, isn't it?"

"Why shouldn't I want to be rich!" retorted Jankin with a trace of the old belligerence.

Before Kate could think of an answer, Geoffrey appeared, walking as though each step was agony. His face was streaked with blood and dirt; his hair and eyebrows were singed.

"I ache all over, but at least I'm alive! Where can we wash?" he asked, wincing as he sat down. "My head still pounds, and I dreamed the whole night long. As though it were all happening again!" He leaned gingerly against a tree. "And I thought that with one thrust of my mighty spear I'd kill that monster! Like St. George. What's this?" he asked, spying the rod beside Jankin. "It looks like the bolt to a crossbow."

"It was sticking out of the trunk of a tree near the bog," replied the cobbler. "It's damaged and warped, but the workmanship is that of a master."

"Sister, look at this! And Tim!"

They examined the weathered shaft with care. It was certainly old and in bad repair. One end was broken, and the inlay—silver and ebony in a familiar pattern—was badly damaged.

"It's like the one Mother . . ." Kate's voice dropped to a whisper. "It's one of the bolts that Grandfather . . ."

"Yes! That Grandfather took with him!"

Jankin listened closely. "Took with him? What do you mean?"

"That Grandfather must've been here during that dragon hunt!" blurted Geoffrey. "Jankin, exactly where was that tree?"

"Right next to the bog. Where you left me. The shaft was sticking out of a knothole. I saw it was well crafted and of costly materials. I wondered how it got there—and who it belonged to. You think it was your grandfather's?"

"It's exactly like the one our mother gave me— the only one she had, for Grandfather had taken the others along. She said it was of rare and precious design—that there were no others like it."

"Does this mean . . . ?" Kate was almost afraid to say it aloud. "Does this mean those hunters long ago also went near the bog?"

"It may, and that they sank to their death . . . just like Fife and Peterkin. Sister, I must find Father. He should be told without delay!" Geoffrey ran off to look for Master Simon.

Kate looked at Tim and tried to still the pounding of her heart.

"In truth, this may be the answer," said Jankin, his voice hushed.

"I pray they suffered less than poor Fife and the mule," said Tim soberly.

Kate nodded, and thought of her mother. How would she receive this news? And—Kate's heart stopped at the thought—was this further reason to believe that there was no dragon of Middlethorpe? But if so, she was alone in harboring such thoughts.

"This is a dragon-haunted place!" burst out Jankin. "I shall be glad to have done with it!"

15

The Unicorn Maid

The hunters were awake. Horses and mules grazed in the lush summer grass. Lances and swords, crossbows and longbows, pitchforks and staves lay scattered on the ground. The dogs, rested and free of their heavy spiked collars, raced about wild with freedom, sore limbs forgotten. Fresh game, shot the day before and left in the clearing, had miraculously still been there, and now was roasting on a spit. Kate was faint with hunger.

Several of the men and Master Simon sat down not far from where she was still sitting with Jankin and Tim.

"I told Father, and he thinks it may be so," exclaimed Geoffrey, coming back to join them. "The hunters may not have been devoured by the monster last time!"

Kate felt a surge of excitement. What did this say about the dragon? "Let's go to Father and the others, and see what they think."

"Shall we go home, Master?" asked one of the

guildsmen as they settled themselves on the ground nearby. "Surely the monster is gone!"

"Vanquished by this maid!" exclaimed another, looking at Kate with wonder. "We fought well, but without the mysterious powder we might all have perished."

"I passed through the place of battle this morning," said Jankin. He looked around the clearing. "This feels different. This has no smell of evil. No sense of danger. Truly, I believe the monster is destroyed!" He pounded his fist in frustration. "If only I had been there to put my spear into the beast!"

"You did right to stay with Fife," said Brother Luke. "But I share your feeling. Yesterday I sensed the presence of evil. All day it was with us. Today this is a place of peace."

"Master!" Rob, filthy with soot, still smeared with blood, approached with Davy, whose injured arm rested in a crude sling. "Where do we clean the men's wounds?"

Master Simon looked up in surprise. "Use the stream! Surely it runs fresh and pure!"

"Master, the dragon was here. The water is fouled."

Kate's heart raced. What should she do? If she told about the unicorn, they would surely mock her. She was no royal maid to be sought out by the mysterious beast! And yet, it was not her alone, but the hunters he had come to protect. And the animals. She would have to speak out. "Brother Luke. Father. Early this morning . . . there was a unicorn in the clearing."

"A unicorn! Here?" Brother Luke stared at her.

"Daughter! What are you saying?" Master Simon spoke sharply.

"At dawn." Kate looked at the stern expression on her father's face, and her courage almost failed her. "I was the only one awake."

"But why did you not say so?" asked Brother Luke. He spoke gently, and Kate relaxed.

"It was all so dreamlike—so unreal."

"Who are we," said the friar, "to know always what is real and what is a dream?"

"I thought no one would believe me. That they would mock me and think me vain."

"I pray you," said Brother Luke, "no one would do such a thing. Tell us about this unicorn."

Kate told all that had happened, and no one laughed. Even Master Simon looked at his daughter with wonder.

"It is a miracle," said the friar. "Indeed, I believe it is a sign to us." He turned to Master Simon. "The men may use the water without fear. The unicorn has purified all foulness with his magical horn." He rose. "I must go for a time to think and pray. Surely the Lord himself is speaking to us."

Kate ran after him. "Brother Luke!"

"What is it, my daughter?"

"You said about the unicorn, What, then, is dream, and what is reality? Are you saying it matters not?"

"I believe the unicorn exists. But, more than that, I believe in its spirit: goodness, love, and virtue. That is the spirit of our Lord himself. And it is more than a dream. More than reality."

"Then what of dragons? Say you the same thing about their evil? Mistress Rose told me she does not believe the monsters are real. That the evil she has seen comes from the souls of men and women—not of dragons. What say you?"

"I believe in the reality of dragons as I do in that of unicorns," said the friar thoughtfully. "I have no reason to doubt their existence. But more than that even, I believe in goodness and evil. I think both exist in this world—in dragons and in unicorns and, yes, in people. I believe that dragons are messengers of Satan. And—dragons or no—the evil of Satan exists. It is evil we must struggle against, no matter where we find it." He regarded her for a moment. "My daughter, we shall speak of this again."

"I thank you," said Kate, "and I shall think on it."

The friar continued to the other side of the clearing. Kate sat down beside the torn and ravaged oak to ponder his words, when she felt a touch on her shoulder.

"May I sit down with you?"

"Father! Here," she said, moving to one side, "this log is thick with moss."

Master Simon lowered his tall frame onto the mossy perch beside her, legs extended. He looked ill at ease.

"These have been astonishing days, my daughter. You have amazed me not once, but many times."

He looked at her and smiled. "It is as though I have never taken the trouble to know my own child."

"Oh, Father! Much that has happened has naught to do with me."

"I wonder," said Master Simon reflectively. "I wonder, indeed. The bringing of the unicorn casket was an act of courage. Not, perhaps, prudent, but certainly brave and ingenious." He shook his head, perplexed. "Not an act I would expect of a . . ."

"Say it, Father!" interrupted Kate with a flash of annoyance. "You would not have expected it of a maid. Am I right?"

Master Simon looked sheepish. "Yes. You are right. And it seems I have been wrong. In more than a few things."

Kate was stunned. Never had her father spoken to her in this way, and for once she was without words. Fortunately, just at that moment there was a cracking of branches at the edge of the forest. Kate clutched him by the arm. "Father, look!" Even as she said it, a figure stepped into the clearing. "Mistress Rose!" Kate sprang to her feet.

Rose had left the fringe of trees. The men around the spit stopped talking and watched as the slight figure with the springing mass of white hair, clad in sandals and robe just like the friar, walked rapidly across the clearing.

"Who is she?"

"What brings this woman to us?"

One of the guildsmen exclaimed, "It's the mad woman! The one who was driven into the forest."

"Take care!" warned someone. "She'll put a curse on us. She's a witch. Remember the last time, and what happened to the hunters!"

Some of the men drew back; others stared, rooted to the ground, overcome with fear. Kate looked at them with dismay. "You're wrong! Mistress Rose is no witch!" She ran to meet her friend with an impulsive embrace. "How I've longed for you!"

"I worried about you, my child," said Mistress Rose. "I had to be sure you were safe. All night long I wondered, and finally I came."

The hunters looked at Rose and at each other. Some of them began to draw near in spite of the warning, eager to see this person—this mad woman—of whom they had heard all their lives.

"Master!" Wat came to Master Simon, who still sat where Kate had left him. "Look! The mad woman has come here, and your daughter is with her. 'Tis not my place to say so, but is that wise?"

"Good Wat, I believe it is," he said, rising to his feet and smiling at the astonished blacksmith. Then he walked toward Kate and Rose. "Kate, my daughter, will you make us known to one another?"

"Oh, Father, this is Mistress Rose. Master Clement told me of her, and that she was a friend of Grandmother Kate's. We met in the forest, and she gave me oatcakes to eat." Kate spoke hurriedly, suddenly terrified her father would send Mistress Rose away, and she would never be able to see her again. "She helped me find the great Druid oak. Without her, I might still be lost."

"I have heard of you, Mistress. I am Simon, a wool merchant, and leader of this hunt. "I bid you welcome," he said gravely.

"Oh, Father," whispered Kate. "Thank you."

"I thank you, Master," said Mistress Rose, "for your welcome."

Brother Luke hurried back from the other side of the clearing, where he had been walking, hands clasped in prayer. "Mistress, we are blessed to have you in our midst!"

"But Friar," protested one of the hunters. "It is the mad woman to whom you speak! The woman who cursed the last hunters and caused their death, and who may be putting her curse on us this very moment!"

"Listen to me, men!" interrupted Master Simon. "Listen with care before you decide about this woman." He pulled the bolt from Grandfather John's crossbow out of his tunic, and held it up for all to see. "Many things have happened to us, things filled with mystery and wonder. This object in my hand is not the least of them. And I have just in these moments heard of it." He turned to Jankin, who had approached with the others. "Tell them, Cobbler, where you found this bolt."

Jankin told them, and then Master Simon explained its meaning. "Men, it says one thing to me. That the men on that doomed expedition sank in the bog, as did Fife and the mule. It's possible they were not devoured by the monster. Exactly what happened remains a mystery, but I do not believe this woman is evil. She cared for my Kate in the forest. And remember well, it was Kate who brought the unicorn horn that slew the monster. Without Mistress Rose we might all be dead! We may very well have banished into the forest a woman who was innocent of the deed for which we condemned her. A woman who is no witch and never placed a curse on anything or anyone." He turned to Mistress Rose. "Welcome her, men, and take her into your midst. She has suffered great wrong at the hands of the people of Middlethorpe. It is time we ask her forgiveness."

"She looks strange in her dress and the wildness of her hair," whispered one of the guildsmen to another. "But not mad, surely."

"Her manner is pleasant, not evil or deranged," replied the other.

Kate explained about their meeting in the forest. Then the hunters came in twos and threes to speak to this strange woman who had come to them out of the forest. Meat was brought from the spit so all could eat, and soon even Davy and the fishmonger, who had been standing apart from the rest, drew near.

"We must decide what to do," said Master Simon as they ate. "It's my sense that we should leave this place and return to our homes. I believe our task is completed—the dragon is truly vanquished. What have your prayers told you, Brother Luke?"

"My brothers and sisters, I believe we have been sent a sign. We know what happened last night. After you had battled with the dragon and exhausted him, this maid drove him off with the magic powder. But there is more. You must listen to her."

Again Kate told of the unicorn in the dawn-lit clearing. When she had finished there was a hush. At last one of the guildsmen spoke. "It is a tale marvelous beyond anything I've heard," he said. "But why, good friar, do you see it as a sign? And to what purpose?"

"The maid was led to us. Even her reason for coming—to bring us the healing horn of the unicorn—was beyond the ordinary. She was guided by the Lord himself, as was the unicorn. Yesterday the dragon was upon us in all his fury, and we were helpless before him. Repeatedly we did battle." He turned to Kate. "But not until you, my daughter, threw the magic powder into his flaming jaws did he retreat."

Brother Luke continued. "I wondered if the monster would yet return, and urged caution. Then, this morning I sensed a change. The smell of evil was gone. But not until I heard her tale was I sure. Do you not see? The monster has departed, and we are at peace!"

Master Simon rose. "Men, as your appointed leader, I declare this dragon hunt at an end! Let us return to our homes!"

The cheering and shouting rang through the forest. The men forgot their bruised and aching bodies, and went leaping about, pounding each other with joy and triumph. The hunt was over! The dragon was vanquished!

"Hail to the unicorn maid!" shouted Rob. And again their voices rang through the clearing. At last they dispersed to wash and clean their wounds, to drink and water the animals, and to prepare for the journey back to Middlethorpe.

"I have brought herbs," said Rose to Master Simon. "If you have need of me, I am at your service."

"You are far better to us than we deserve!" exclaimed Master Simon. "That you should help those who drove you away and ignored you all these years!"

"Let us forget the past," she replied. "Your Kate has helped melt some of the bitterness in my heart."

"Geoffrey needs your help," said Master Simon, "and Davy and Rob, as well as many others. And some of the animals are cut and bleeding."

"Bring them to me," she said. "It has been far too long since I've used what skills I possess." She looked at Kate, who was standing beside her in a kind of happy trance. "Perhaps I can teach your daughter some of the things her grandmother first taught me."

"You are a blessing for all of us, Mistress," said Master Simon as he turned to leave.

"Well, my dear," said Rose, taking Kate by the arm, "it seems that many things have happened since we parted in the forest." Gently she pulled Kate down beside her onto a mossy log.

"Oh, Mistress Rose, many many things!" Kate told

her everything, and frowned. "I really thought for a moment that I saw the dragon in the forest. In the flames and heat he seemed to be there right in the midst of us. But then—after the rain put out the fire, when I looked again—all I saw was charred branches and trees." She leaned toward Rose. "With the flames, it would have looked just like the monster! I don't know what to think!"

Rose stared at her. "It is as I thought, my child. Just as I've always thought about the dragon. The storms, and the noise and lightning and rain—the heat and fire. The frightening, dark, forbidding forest. The foul stench of the reeking bog. It is as I've always believed! But when I once mentioned it, people were not glad to be free of their fear—their fear of the terrible monster who haunted their lives. They were angry because I dared have such thoughts!"

"Brother Luke believes the monster exists, Mistress Rose. But he was not surprised or angry when I asked him about it. Nor when I asked whether he thinks the unicorn is real. Most of all, he believes that evil is real—and goodness, as well."

"I agree with him there, in any case," said Mistress Rose. "Later, when all this is past, you will know what to do. In the meantime, remember that you may be struggling with a great and powerful truth. Sometime, perhaps, many many years from now—not in my lifetime, or in yours—people will no longer be in terror of dragons. Then they can struggle against other evils."

"But is it not untruthful? They think of me as the unicorn maid, and vanquisher of the dragon. And I'm not sure it is as they think."

"Whatever the truth," said Mistress Rose, "evil has been vanquished by good. Whether it was a dragon, or whether love came through the mysterious unicorn, who is to say? The important thing is we are at peace again, and evil has been driven back into the darkness."

Thank you! If only I could see you all the time!"

"Perhaps now things will change, and the people of Middlethorpe will no longer create a gulf between us. Look! Here comes your father with some of the men. I must get to work, and you can help me." She pulled a bundle of herbs out of the bag at her waist and handed it to Kate. "If this, then, is to be your calling, it is time you began."

Together they spread out the ointments and herbs. Together they cleaned cuts and bruises, made poultices, and bound up wounds with strips of linen. At last, when everyone had been cared for, when all had washed, and drunk their fill, they set out on their journey, following the little stream which, Rose told them, would merge with Beechwood Brook and lead them home.

16

Home

They had left the clearing at noon the day before, and had ridden until sundown. At dawn they had continued, stopping only to eat the last of their provisions. Jankin and Brother Luke had accompanied Rose to her home in the forest.

"This place is now where I belong," she had said to Kate, embracing her as she made ready to leave. "But I shall miss you sorely."

"Mistress Rose!" Kate had cried. "When shall I see you again?"

"I don't know," Rose had replied, "but it may be sooner than we thought."

"I shall visit you in the forest," said Kate, suddenly filled with joy and a sense of assurance. "Master Clement and I will seek you out."

The hunters had gathered to bid farewell to Mistress Rose. "I'll not forget you—nor your welcome to me," she said to them. "And I will surely come to Middlethorpe to visit all who are now my friends." Then she had gone with Jankin and Brother Luke, who were coming back the following day to give the innkeeper a proper burial before returning home.

Kate rode on the chestnut, seated behind Geoffrey, as on the day their mother had caught her out in the market square. How long ago that seemed! Tim had been just behind them, but they had not been able to talk, for most of the time the woods were dense, and they had ridden in single file. But Kate and Geoffrey had whiled away the time reliving everything that had occurred. Now, nearing the end of the journey, Kate summoned up the courage to ask the question that consumed her.

"Brother, have you ever wondered if the dragon is real?"

"Real? What do you mean? Of course he's real!"

"How can you be certain?"

Geoffrey turned in his saddle and stared at her. "You saw him! I saw you running from him! I heard your cries for help!"

"Sh-sh-sh. You're right. I did think that I saw him. But the fire was scorching hot, and my head was in a whirl. Later, after the downpour, I wondered."

"But you saw the dragon with your own eyes! He killed two men and the mule. And he almost killed me! If it hadn't been for you and that unicorn powder, I'd be dead this moment! How can you even think he's not real? Are you mad?"

Kate shook her head with impatience. "Why can't you understand? I'm not sure. Could it have been the storm and heat of fire? Not once was anyone able to touch him or pierce his side. He was all shadows and smoke. And flame."

"But when you threw that casket he was gone! And he's not returned. What of that?"

"But did you see what remained? Branches and trees all in a sodden heap. And you in the middle! It could have been fire and leaping flame, falling trees, and pouring rain. Nothing more."

"Kate!" Geoffrey shook his head. "Sometimes I think you're truly mad!"

"Why?"

"I'll tell you why. You shouldn't say such things, or you'll end up like that Mad Rose. Besides, why should it matter? He's gone. Whatever he is, he's gone! And, thanks to you, I live!"

Kate was silent. Why continue? But she couldn't forget the words of Mistress Rose. That men and women were terrified of something that didn't exist! Was it possible? Maybe the forest would no longer be dreaded if people understood there was nothing to fear. Kate rubbed her aching head. If only she could puzzle things out!

Suddenly she saw the light of the meadow ahead.

"Brother, we're home!"

As the chestnut followed the other animals out into the sunlight, Kate could see past the village and on to the oak grove where Tim and his master had their workplace. Beyond, on the long green slope near Lord Hugo's barley fields, a row of pennants fluttered in the breeze. They marked the fairgrounds, and the highroad was filled with people and carts and animals all streaming toward them. Was it possible the Middlethorpe Fair had begun with the hunters still gone?

"Listen!" Geoffrey halted the mare. "They've seen us!"

Suddenly Kate heard the cathedral bells. She looked across the fields and there, streaming through the gates to welcome them, was the entire population of town and village.

"Brother, let's meet them! Tim!" she called. "Come with us!"

"I'll see you later," he called back over his shoulder, already riding off to the welcoming crowd. "My master's come to meet me, and I must go to him."

"Look!" yelled Geoffrey, spurring the mare, "I see Mother." Master Simon had seen her too, and in moments the four of them were reunited.

Home at last, Kate rushed to her room and searched under the coverlet. And, yes, the dragon parchment was still there, the spiky beast fierce as ever. She stared at the little drawing, and ran her finger along the lashing tail. What was the truth? she wondered. Would she ever know?

The fair had not begun, but everything was ready, waiting only for the hunters' return. It was to open that very afternoon with a festive procession. But first, Goodwife Barbara gathered everyone for a meal to celebrate the safe return of her husband and children. Master Clement was there, still weak, but regaining his strength. Rob had come with Daisy and little Robin. The only one missing, thought Kate, was Tim. But she knew he would be in the procession. The feast was a triumph, and by the time the last fruit pie was gone, the last cup of spiced wine emptied, the gathered company knew all there was to tell.

"We thought you had been destroyed!" burst out Goodwife Barbara. "Devoured by the dragon! The forest was rent with lightning and bright with fire! We had given you up for dead!"

"Had it not been for you, Goodwife," said Daisy, "I think I would have died of fear." She sat clutching little Robin and grasping Rob by the arm as though she would never let him out of her sight again.

"Tell me, my daughter," said Master Clement, "was the unicorn as I said? Milk-white and proud, with a horn that spirals from the middle of its forehead?"

"Just as you said, Master," replied Kate.

"Was it beautiful beyond imagining?" asked the old man.

"More beautiful than I can possibly say."

"It should be written down," declared Master Clement. "Now, while you remember it just as it happened."

Kate sighed. "Geoffrey can do it. But I can't even read, much less write."

"Geoffrey could do it for part of the adventure," said the apothecary. "But the unicorn—no one saw it but you. In Paris," he continued, addressing Master Simon, "there is a famous noblewoman who writes books. And in other places young maids from the towns—maids just like Kate—are being taught. This may be the moment," he said to Kate, "if you will permit me."

She nodded, unable to speak for the lump in her throat.

"Your Kate has a gift for the healing herbs, and a love for them," said the apothecary to Master Simon and Goodwife Barbara. "I am an old man, now much weakened. I need someone to be my helper. Dear friends, let Kate be my apprentice. She will learn about the healing arts, and be a blessing to Middle-thorpe. And as she learns about herbs and roots and berries, she shall learn about reading and writing, as well."

"Father, pay heed to the master! My sister should learn to read and write." Kate listened to Geoffrey in amazement. "I'm being taught," he continued, "but it gives me no pleasure. Kate burns to read, and why should she not learn? Because she is a maid? Father, such thinking is out of date!"

Master Simon made no comment, and Kate held her breath. "Perhaps you are right," he said at last, with a sigh. Kate was weak with relief, then newly apprehensive as he continued. "But it has always been improper, to my thinking. Reading is the realm of monks and scholars, not of women! Still," he said, shaking his head in wonder, and looking at his daughter as though he had never seen her before, "after what I have seen of my Kate during these past few days, I think she may be one of those who should be taught. What think you, my dear?" he asked, turning to his wife.

Goodwife Barbara chuckled. "As you are one so angered by the posturing of the nobles, and always in search of the new and advanced, I should think you would want your daughter to be among the first young maids to read. As for being Master Clement's apprentice," she continued, "it would strike me as unseemly and impossible except for one thing." She turned to the old man. "Any time spent with one so wise and good can only be a blessing for our Kate."

"Oh, Mother!" Kate clasped her mother's hand, then hurried to Master Clement and clasped his. "Oh, thank you! Father, I'll make a book for you with the whole tale of the dragon and the unicorn. A small one with a cover of wood, so you may carry it with you on your travels. Geoffrey, will you help?"

"If I can." He grinned. "Perhaps for once I'll be happy about my studies. But now we must hurry, or we'll be late for the procession. You are to be an honored guest."

"Whatever did you mean," asked Kate, as they hurried to the town square, "that I was to be an honored guest?"

"You're already famed as the unicorn maid!"

"Geoffrey, now you're the one who's mad," said Kate, feeling uncomfortable. "People won't remember for longer than the end of the fair." She looked up at him. "But I'll never forget how you spoke up for me with Father."

"I'll never forget that you saved my life," replied Geoffrey. "And I truly don't think you're mad, no matter what strange ideas you hatch." He grinned at her, and Kate thought she had never felt so close to her brother.

They caught up with Master Simon and Rob, who were also to be in the procession. When they reached the square, Kate mounted a horse that had been readied for her, and they waited to be lined up in proper order. First came Lord Hugo and Lady Constance. Then the abbot and the burgesses, followed by special visitors. At the end, headed by Kate as the unicorn maid, came the dragon hunters in double file. The townspeople cheered. Kate looked into the crowd and waved at her mother and Daisy. Robin, wild with excitement, was riding in the procession with his father.

Kate turned in her saddle to face Tim, whose horse was directly behind her own. "Tim, I'm going to learn about herbs and plants from Master Clement. I'll be an apprentice, just like you!"

Tim stared. "And you'll never cease to amaze me! First, you say you're going on the dragon hunt, and you actually do it! Then you manage to rid us of the dragon with the unicorn powder. And now, you're going to be the first maid I've known who's an apprentice!"

"There's something else! I'll learn to read with Master Clement. Father said I could! And when I learn to write, I'll make a book for him telling everything that happened in the forest. Then he can read it on his travels. And Tim," she hurried on, "when you make the windows for the Cathedral, will you make one that shows the dragon and the unicorn?"

Tim's eyes sparked with interest as he considered the idea. "If I have the skill, and if my master lets me, yes. Will you, then, make something for me?"

"What can I make? I have no skills."

"When you set down for your father the tale of the dragon and unicorn, will you set it down for me, as well?"

"Oh, Tim, yes!" She thought for a moment. "Can you make pictures for it with beautiful colors?"

Tim's face glowed. "I will, and when I do, we'll really have done something together. Not like Daisy's jug and flowers, which only seemed that way."

Kate remembered that moment at Daisy's feast when they had looked at the jug. It had been the beginning of something. And that something was continuing to unfold.

"Someday I'd like to learn reading from you, as well," said Tim. He ran his fingers through his hair and blushed. "I approve of maids who can read."

"And I approve of men who make beautiful things out of glass," said Kate in a rush, "and who can make music and pictures." What was happening to her? Kate hadn't known that one could be so happy. She remembered Tim still didn't know what Mistress Rose had said about dragons, and she longed to tell him. There was so much to talk about!

But now there was no time, because the hunting horns began to sound, and the colorful procession started through the narrow streets out to the meadow that had been the site of the Middlethorpe Fair for as long as anyone could remember. They streamed through the gates, pennants fluttering, trumpets calling, bagpipes shrilling. Kate felt she was part of a bright, glittering serpent that wound its way toward the long slope, alive with tents and people and animals, all under a brilliant sky. She looked across the meadows to the dark line of the forest. There she had seen a different kind of serpent—one she would ponder as long as she lived. But right now the monster seemed remote, and she was glad to think of other things.

The procession reached the fairgrounds. Lord Hugo's opening speech was finally at an end. Moments later, Kate, laughing with Tim and Geoffrey, and pulling little Robin by the hand, mingled with the crowds that surged past the tents and food stalls, the mimes and jugglers, the prancing dogs and dancing bears and endless diversions of the wonderful Middlethorpe Fair.